MW01616790

ARRIVALS AND DEPARTURES

ARRIVALS AND DEPARTURES

A NOVEL

AMANDA EYRE WARD

BALLANTINE BOOKS

New York

Ballantine Books
An imprint of Random House
A division of Penguin Random House LLC
1745 Broadway, New York, NY 10019
randomhousebooks.com
penguinrandomhouse.com

Hardcover ISBN 978-0-593-50032-3
Ebook ISBN 978-0-593-50033-0

Printed in the United States of America
1st Printing
First Edition

BOOK TEAM: Production editor: Andy Lefkowitz • Managing editor: Pamela Alders •
Production manager: Angela McNally • Copy editor: Kathryn Jones •
Proofreaders: Dan Goff, Barbara Jatkola, Olivia Johnson, Robin Slutzky, and Barbara Stussy

Book design by Debbie Glasserman

The authorized representative in the EU for product safety and compliance is
Penguin Random House Ireland, Morrison Chambers, 32 Nassau Street,
Dublin D02 YH68, Ireland. https://eu-contact.penguin.ie

THANK YOU, HEATHER QUIRK-COURTS,
FOR GETTING ME THROUGH A LONG WINTER IN ATHENS . . .
FOR EASTER MORNING ON THE ACROPOLIS . . .
FOR BEING MY TRUE FRIEND.

A NOTE FROM THE AUTHOR

Arrivals and Departures depicts the highs and lows of bipolar and related disorders, which can include suicidal ideation. My goal in exploring Lee's mental illness is for readers who wrestle with mood disorders to feel seen, and to know that they are not alone. If you or a loved one is suffering from a mood regulation disorder, please reach out to your medical professional. There is hope, there is help, there is light.

ARRIVALS AND DEPARTURES

Every time I ever said, I want to die
I meant I am willing to do anything to live.

—ANDREA GIBSON

I was much further out than you thought
And not waving but drowning.

—STEVIE SMITH

PROLOGUE

ON THE MORNING OF MY DEPARTURE, I BUY A COFFEE AT CAFÉ YIA-semi. They know me here now, and I'm left alone when I sit on the patio to work. I'm sure the locals think I'm strange—an American woman with a big scrapbook and a small pair of scissors. Glue sticks and a faraway gaze. Sometimes I close my eyes. Maybe people think I'm sleeping, but I'm creating art in my mind—moving images around, cropping them, seeing how the colors line up.

With my eyes closed, anything is possible.

Money is becoming a problem. My family could help, but I don't want to hear their opinions about my choices, so I don't ask.

Beautiful books are expensive, as are supplies, classes, and medical emergencies. But I've kept us afloat, one day at a time. I don't need anyone's help or judgment.

He is the only one who sees me as I am: creative, beautiful, someone who matters. What could be more important? For my trip, I pack cotton dresses and sandals. I paint my toes. It feels frightening to leave my new home and head to an island in the middle of the ocean. I was not raised to take risks.

His belief in me has given me courage—to become an artist, to splurge on myself. We text as I lock up my apartment, as I hail a taxi. I can hardly believe this day is finally here. All my dreams are coming true, at last, at last. I can already envision the collage I will create: photographs of the beach, remnants from evenings of wine and laughter. Images of me—for once—ablaze. A wooden table with a paper cloth, candles, plates of grilled vegetables, my own bare feet in blue water.

It's not until I am over the ocean that my phone trills, the first warning:

My love, there is a problem.

1 FLORA

Girls, I am headed off to my Santorini collage workshop!!! Love you both so, so much and I will be home on Sunday by lunchtime. You can order pizza and get what you need with my credit card but be cheap!
Love, love, love, love, Mom.

Their apartment in Athens, Greece, felt empty—emptier than usual. Flora wished she could bike over to her Grammy Charlotte's house the way she'd done when they lived in the same gated community in Savannah, Georgia. Grammy kept a pantry of snacks for Flora and her sister: Nutter Butters, Mallomars, off-brand Chex mix, nuts. Flora would sit on a tall stool at Grammy's kitchen counter and talk about whatever and Grammy would listen.

Something's wrong with my mom, Flora could say.

Or Flora and her grandmother could take Grammy Charlotte's golf cart to the Palmetto Club. Flora knew her grandmother's member number—P1107—and Flora could order ice cream or a basket of curly fries. They could sit on lounge chairs by the pool and Flora could tell Grammy Charlotte she had a very bad feeling.

A mint chocolate chip cone. The smell of chlorine, sunscreen, and fries. Grammy Charlotte in some bright-colored visor, turning to Flora when Flora said, *Grammy?*

What is it, honey?

Grammy Charlotte, Flora could say, *Mom's in trouble. Please help us. We're all alone, and I'm scared.*

2 LEE

LEE PERKINS ADJUSTED HER OVERSIZED GUCCI SUNGLASSES AND raised her drink for another sip, but there was nothing in her cup. Oh, she remembered the days when the gentleman who served Perrier-Jouët to the Beverly Hills Hotel pool cabanas would fill her champagne flute without Lee even noticing it was drained!

"Do you want another chardonnay, dear?"

Reluctantly, Lee lowered her gaze to her mother, Charlotte, who sat next to her at the Palmetto Club, a community pool located just a quick golf cart ride from Charlotte's house. Charlotte wore a zebra-striped bathing suit; a matching zebra-striped visor; and Candy Yum Yum–colored lipstick she'd "borrowed" from her daughter and never returned.

"Yes," said Lee.

"Hurry up, then, and get me one too," said Charlotte. "Drinks are half-price 'til six! Wine Down Wednesday, you know."

Lee rose from a luxuriant slouch, wincing at the Savannah sunlight cutting through her faded umbrella. She was not surrounded by movie producers, A-list stars, and Hollywood influencers. No: Lee was forty-three years old, formerly famous, and living in her mother's guest room, sleeping underneath a hideous painting of bulldogs on a sailboat.

Her napkin read: TRUTH VERSUS CHARDONNAY.

Lee and her mother chose chardonnay. Every time.

After a few, Lee could pretend she was back in golden California. She could return to the time when her bank accounts were flush and her family wasn't scattered across the world, each one rapidly disappearing into their own private catastrophes.

As Lee strolled toward the snack bar, retirees pretended not to stare at Charlotte Perkins's "troubled" daughter, the reality TV star and mental patient about whom they said, not so sotto voce, *Lee Perkins is a complete disaster but wow, isn't she gorgeous?*

Lee felt as if she were disappearing, her career stalled and her manic depression muffled—but not eradicated—by medications that narrowed her range of emotions and made her hands shake.

Honestly, thought Lee, everyone in her family seemed to be adrift. Charlotte rarely drove her car outside Palmetto Shores, her gated community. Lee's brother, Cord, was drowning in booze and work. Regan, Lee's baby sister, had moved all the way to Greece where she lived with her teenaged daughters, Isabelle and Flora, on the glittering Mediterranean Sea. Lee had once underlined sentences in a novel that described her family: *When you are small, if you reach out, and nobody takes your hand, you stop reaching out, and reach inside, instead. That's just the way it was.*

Lee and her siblings had been raised in the late 1980s, a time of big hair and enough Aqua Net to hold it in place. A time (especially in the American South) of preppy vibes and straight teeth; cold smiles that betrayed nothing, L.L.Bean totes, and living by the credo—later cemented in the movie *The Wolf of Wall Street*— "Act as if!"

What happened to adults who knew only how to *act as if* they were a family? Over the next few weeks, in New York and Savannah and Athens, Greece, the furiously flailing Perkins family would sink, one by one. And in their last breaths, could they, could Lee—lovely, sad Lee—see that what would save them was quiet, unsexy, and hidden in plain sight? A simple truth, yet hard to understand: If you didn't reach out, you would never know you weren't alone in the water.

3 FLORA

ON THEIR SECOND NIGHT ALONE, FLORA AND HER SISTER, ISABELLE, made noodles with butter for dinner—the weird, square χυλοπίτες noodles, the butter tangier than American Land O'Lakes. "I know you think I'm paranoid," said Flora, wiping her lips with a paper napkin, "but I just have a bad feeling about Mom and this craft workshop. When I checked her location, I couldn't find her on my list. She disabled Find My!"

"You're tracking Mom now?" Isabelle raised an eyebrow. She had twisted her long hair into a topknot and wore very expensive sweatpants, a shirt with an illustration of a vintage red Ford Bronco and the swirled letters AMERICAN CLASSIC, and Nike Air Force 1s. She was a stunning and volatile eighteen-year-old, unpredictable and sometimes mean, but Flora adored her and clung to her in a way Flora knew made her sister angry.

"And I sent her a text and it didn't show delivered or read, Isabelle. Something's wrong."

"I'm sure it's fine," said Isabelle, scrolling. "Just let her have her weirdo artist retreat, Jesus."

"I think we should call Grammy Charlotte."

"Oh my God, I miss Palmetto Shores! I miss the club and the

golf cart and even the creepy dog painting in Grammy's guest room."

Flora smiled. "Where did she even get that painting?" she said.

"Why would bulldogs be sailing a boat?"

"They have little sailor hats!" exclaimed Flora.

"And Grammy always has food for us. The whole closet pantry full."

"I was just thinking about that—Mallomars!"

"And those mini ice cream sandwiches in her freezer," said Isabelle, stretching her arms on the table and putting her head down in dramatic anguish. "Whyyyyy did we move here?"

"Do you really think Mom's OK?"

"Nobody's OK, Flor. But I'm sure she'll text you back. Don't call the police just yet."

"I'm just worried."

"You're always worried," said Isabelle.

She said it kindly.

For once, Isabelle was being kind.

4 LEE

ON THE SUNLIGHT-YELLOW COUCH IN CHARLOTTE'S LIVING ROOM,
Charlotte and Lee ate Triscuits and a wedge of cheddar for dinner
while they watched *Trafficked with Mariana van Zeller*. The night
grew lavender outside the sliding glass doors, sprinklers misting
the golf course with a hushing sound. Above the fireplace, there
was a portrait of Charlotte with her children. They looked young,
beautiful, and scared.

Lee texted her agent, Francine: any news?

Trying my best! Maybe do something on YouTube?

Do WHAT on YouTube?

When Francine did not respond, Lee said, "Mom, I'm going
to go call my agent."

"Ooooh, that's exciting! Good luck, dear," said Charlotte, nibbling a Triscuit.

Francine answered on the third ring. "Do *what* on YouTube?"
Lee repeated.

"Honestly, I don't know what," said Francine. "It's just an
idea. People are TikToking all over town."

"I am an actor, Francine," said Lee. "Though I do love *Trafficked with Mariana van Zeller*. Could I do a show like *Trafficked
with Mariana van Zeller*?"

"Mariana van Zeller is a trained journalist," said Francine. "But maybe you could . . . I don't know . . . go choose a bikini and TikTok about it? I've got to run. Talk soon. Ciao ciao!"

Reclining on her mother's guest room bed, Lee contemplated the bulldog painting. Where had her mother picked up this awful picture? Who would devote hours of their life to creating such a monstrosity? Why bulldogs? Why a sailboat?

Lee did not need to turn her head to see the dark shadow, her constant companion. Depression quoted Francine: *Go choose a bikini and TikTok about it.*

Eight months ago, Lee had been a reality TV star. She'd loved the attention, the money, and the sense that she'd found her purpose. She bought Charlotte a new golf cart. She helped her sister, Regan, move all her children and crap to Athens after Regan took a Vision Board Workshop that convinced Regan her real life would only begin when she moved to Greece. She invited her brother, Cord, to the American Reality Television Awards. (He said no and she lost the Reality Queen Award to one of the sister wives.)

Life, for a while there, was sweet!

But, of course, darkness (Lee's old friend) came to talk to her again.

When Lee noticed that her depression had returned—a black shadow—it was as if it had been there all along, and would always be there. Depression had soaked beside Lee in the hot tub of her Hollywood Hills rental, enjoyed martinis at the Frolic Room, lay down on the kitchen floor right next to Lee when her agent, Francine, called to tell her that her reality show, *One of You to Love Me,* had been canceled.

After the call, Lee had stayed in her pajamas for ten days, then changed into the cheap cotton sweatsuit they gave her at the Stewart and Lynda Resnick Neuropsychiatric Hospital at UCLA.

At the hospital, Lee befriended a fellow depressive named Remington. "Like the pistol I put in my mouth," Remington said, when they were introduced. "Didn't pull the trigger, though." Remington had memorized passages from the book *Infinite Jest*. Lee had to agree that the author of *Infinite Jest*, who had eventually succeeded in ending his life, knew what depression felt like. For example: "These worst mornings with cold floors and hot windows and merciless light—the soul's certainty that the day will have to be not traversed but sort of climbed, vertically, and then that going to sleep again at the end of it will be like falling, again, off something tall and sheer." Remington performed this passage as a soliloquy in the Community Room, then said, "Right?"

Lee and her cohorts nodded, stunned at being known.

Eventually, they found the right medications to somewhat stabilize Lee, though Depression did not disappear. It was quiet sometimes, but then would speak so loudly it seemed like fact.

Lee's doctors had suggested she stay with "trusted family" when she left the hospital, so Lee went to her mom's house to recover. Charlotte had a Zoom call with Lee's medical team, and they advised Charlotte lock up Lee's medications to avoid an overdose.

"Yoo-hoo!" Lee's mom appeared in the doorway, a large goblet of wine in each hand. "I brought you a teensy splash," she said. "And it's time for your pills."

"Thanks, Mom," said Lee. "It's also time for your pills."

"But mine aren't for my *brain*," said Charlotte, meanly.

"Mom!" Lee felt the familiar surge of resentment.

"My brain is just fine," noted Charlotte.

Lee almost laughed. Neither of their brains was fine. The difference was, Lee knew it. She also knew she was being unfair. Charlotte had her own ways of surviving. But right now, Lee didn't have the energy to be generous.

Depression spoke clearly: *The sleeping pills are in your mom's medicine cabinet. You can take the whole bottle tonight, say goodbye, and be free.*

Part of her—a small, stubborn part—knew that Depression was wrong. But despite her meds, that voice was fainter every day, and Depression's instructions louder: *Just get the pills. Then you have an option, the possibility of relief.*

Lee battled Depression every hour, every minute, she was awake. Nobody knew how hard she fought—it was like holding a door shut against tremendous force. If she swallowed all her sleeping pills, the door would slam open and knock Lee flat. Then, at last, she could rest.

"Cheers, Lee Lee!" Mother and daughter clinked their goblets and reclined on the bed. The Savannah moon was beautiful outside the window. Lee could hear cicadas calling.

5 CHARLOTTE

CHARLOTTE SAT NEXT TO HER ELDEST DAUGHTER, GAZED AT THE SA-
vannah moon, and sipped her chardonnay. Her mind wandered
to her last good kiss, or honestly her last kiss *period*. It was, of
course, her goodbye kiss with Paros, her Greek love.

Her Greek *lover*.

Was it possible that Paros was still alive when her own bones
were so fragile that Dr. Maloney's nurse compared them to paper
chopsticks? ("Like the ones you get at Panda Express, you know?"
she had added, unnecessarily. Rude!) The memory of Charlotte's
goodbye kiss with Paros was clear in her mind, unlike many
things these days.

Charlotte had fallen for Paros during a Mediterranean cruise.
She'd hoped to keep the romance going, but Paros visited the US
just once. He had worn his farmer-ish clothing—jeans and dark
button-downs—and she took him to the Hilton Head outlet mall
to buy him pastel pants and a collared shirt from the Ralph Lauren outlet. The next day, Paros requested a walk in downtown
Savannah. Charlotte drove him to Chippewa Square, her favorite.
It was surrounded by several large oak trees that provided a bit of
shade. She found a parking spot on Abercorn and they wandered
across the wide square, dodging tourists, to a bench.

"What is that called?" said Paros, pointing to the Spanish moss that hung from the branches of old oak trees, draping them like tattered gray shawls. Charlotte told him, explaining that the bromeliads used the trees to get closer to the sun. Paros took this in, then went to read the placard on the statue of James Oglethorpe. Paros was much more interested in history than Charlotte—why dwell on the past?

Yet here she was—dwelling!—remembering Paros turning from the statue toward Charlotte, then shocking her by kneeling down and asking Charlotte to marry him, to return with him to his Greek farm on an island she couldn't remember the name of. "I can't move to America," said Paros. "You understand? I can't leave my land." His land? Charlotte was sure it was lovely, but Paros had told her that his nearest grocery store was a ten-minute drive away. As for golf courses? Outlet malls? Nope. "I can take care of you on my island, Charlotte," he had said, his voice tender.

She said yes, but very quietly, and he fitted a chintzy ring with a diamond chip on her finger.

The next day, Paros was due to fly home. On the way to the airport, he chatted gaily about how he would prepare the farm for her arrival. But the more Paros spoke about getting a new oven and something about a bed made of horsehair, the more Charlotte acknowledged internally that there was just no way in H-E-double hockey sticks.

After she told him she'd changed her mind and handed him back the sparkly little ring, he'd kissed her passionately, then said, "Don't call me ever again."

"But why?"

"My heart is fully broken," said Paros.

At the time, this had seemed a bit dramatic. A decade later, Charlotte was forced to acknowledge that she, too, was heartbroken. She'd tried to be numb, move on, but honestly, it hadn't worked.

Had Paros married again? Charlotte imagined the olive groves he'd described to her, the way (he'd said) the air smelled of sea, the taste of the thyme honey from his beehives. "Oh, Paros," she murmured. Was he alive? Did he think of her?

"What, Mom?" said Lee.

"Nothing," said Charlotte.

The past could not be changed.

6 FLORA

SIXTEEN WAS A WEIRD AGE TO BE, THOUGHT FLORA. ON THE ONE hand, she was old enough to drive—if she had learned to drive, which she had not—but on the other hand, she still needed a mom. She needed *her* mom, but now it had been *three days* since her mom had left Athens for her artist retreat on Santorini, and Flora was honestly starting to freak out. Her mom's note had said she would be home by Sunday and OK, it was only Friday, but Flora had never gone this long without speaking to her mom. Ever.

She'd explained the situation to the White Hat Hacking Club. Her friends agreed that disabling Find My was bad.

"Nobody disables Find My," said Nico. "Especially not parents who don't know what it is."

"And don't forget all the stuff we found out about her boyfriend," added Maya.

"*Alleged* boyfriend," said Flora.

"Right," said Maya.

"Something is definitely up," said Nico.

Flora nodded. She knew it. But what was Flora supposed to do? After White Hat Hacking Club, she took the metro back to Plaka, trying to convince herself her mom was fine. Maybe Regan had put her phone in airplane mode for her retreat? Maybe she'd lost it? And would walk in any minute saying, "Can you get over the light in this city?"

Flora's mom was obsessed with the light in Athens. She had basically packed them up and brought them across the world so she could drink tea and gaze out the window of their weensy apartment at sunset and say, "It's like the whole city is the color of a tangerine!"

Although, to be honest, her mom hadn't mentioned the light in a while.

Flora could call her dad, Matt, but he was useless; and also, Flora was glad he couldn't hurt them anymore.

There was her famous Auntie Lee . . . but Flora had learned early that Aunt Lee was fragile and shouldn't be burdened. The adults in Savannah had always whispered about Lee's latest crisis— another breakup, another hospitalization, another time Lee was "going through something."

"Don't bother Auntie Lee," Mom would say. "She needs her space."

Flora saw her sister on their balcony, a wide slab where Regan had positioned three chairs she'd refinished in bright colors. The balcony overlooked the street below, and was maybe Flora's favorite place in Athens, although, hold on, it was a tie between the balcony and the Starbucks in Syntagma Square.

Isabelle was at the edge, ashing her cigarette over the wrought-iron railing. When their mom wasn't home, Isabelle smoked Davidoff Slims, imported from Switzerland. The cigarettes' gold package had a label with big black letters: SMOKING KILLS.

Flora slid open the door. "You're not supposed to smoke," she said, knowing she sounded like a stupid narc but not honestly even caring. "It's really bad for you, Isabelle."

"Oh, zip it," said Isabelle. "Stupid narc."

"I'm not a stupid narc!"

"Sorry," said Isabelle. "I'm sorry. And honestly, Flor? Don't start smoking. When I'm not smoking, it's, like . . . all I can think about is when I *can* smoke. I hate it. I'm already addicted to something and I'm only eighteen."

"That's bad," said Flora.

"I know," said Isabelle, and then she drew in on her Davidoff dramatically and exhaled smoke even more dramatically.

"Have you heard anything from Mom?"

"She's *fine*," said Isabelle dismissively.

"But why would she disable Find My?"

"Fuck if I know," said Isabelle. Flora winced at the swear. Who was Isabelle trying to impress?

"Find My doesn't just disable itself," insisted Flora.

"I don't know what to tell you," said Isabelle. "Maybe it does, and you're not as smart as you think."

Flora looked at her boots, kicked one with the other one. "I'm hungry," she said. "Do you think we can order some pizza?"

"You've got Mom's Apple Pay. Go ahead."

Flora had been hoping that Isabelle would order the pizza, now that she was home for once. Isabelle was always out with her friends and her stunning-but-scary girlfriend, Anastasia, who had instructed Isabelle to switch from American Spirits (the coolest at Savannah Country Day School) to Davidoffs. (Everything cool in America was gauche here in Greece.) Flora was lonely.

"Do you want me to order?" said Isabelle, her tone mocking. "And put out plates and napkins for you?" Despite the fact that Isabelle was making fun of her, Flora was grateful.

"Yes," she admitted.

Isabelle put out her cigarette in a pot of blooming azaleas that Flora and her mom had planted when they moved in. "OK," said Isabelle. But instead of moving, Isabelle was still for a moment.

She put both her hands on the balcony railing. Flora watched in horror as Isabelle's bone-thin shoulders began to shudder. Isabelle made a strangled sound: She was crying.

"Isabelle?" said Flora. Seeing her brash sister in tears was a nightmare. "Isabelle!" she said, jumping up and rushing to her sister.

Isabelle shoved her away. "I hate being all alone here," said Isabelle, not looking at Flora. In a tender, wavering voice, Isabelle said, "I hate her. I hate her for leaving us alone here!"

Flora's heart was beating way too fast, her chest tightening. "Don't hate her," whispered Flora. "Please don't hate her."

Isabelle whirled around. "Why isn't she texting us back?" she said. "And what even is this ridiculous note?" She threw her mother's goodbye note at Flora. Isabelle had crumpled the note in her fist; Flora smoothed the paper and read it for the hundredth time:

Girls, I am headed off to my Santorini collage workshop!!! Love you both so, so much and I will be home on Sunday by lunchtime. You can order pizza and get what you need with my credit card but be cheap!
Love, love, love, love, Mom.

"I'm calling Grammy Charlotte," said Flora.

7 LEE

CHARLOTTE HAD A WALL PHONE. IT RANG THROUGHOUT THE DAY AND night, a reminder that Charlotte couldn't be trusted with credit cards. She'd run up tabs at Neiman Marcus, the Gap outlet, the Ralph Lauren outlet, BleuBelle, the Paris Brocade, HomeGoods, Bed Bath & Beyond, J.Crew, Old Navy, and Michaels arts and crafts store.

"Michaels?" Lee exclaimed, peering at Charlotte's stack of unpaid bills. "What on earth, Mom?" Lee was irritable: She'd crept to her mother's medicine cabinet in the middle of the night to discover that Charlotte had hidden Lee's pills elsewhere. Her mother knew Lee was listening to Depression's entreaties. Of course she knew—Charlotte had always been sharper than she let on when it came to her children's self-destruction.

"I wanted to decorate for the holidays!" said Charlotte now.

"What holiday is in April?" said Lee. "Wait, is Easter in April?"

"Yes, Easter is in April," said Charlotte, who had become less religious as soon as Father Thomas, Charlotte's decade-long crush, had moved to a diocese in Cleveland. "But I was buying decorations for *next Christmas*. Everything was fifty percent off—garlands, candles, faux pine needles. Nothing tacky."

Lee set the bills aside. Her mother had become one of those

people who hang flags keyed to the season outside their front door. There was currently a flag featuring April flowers rippling in the wind outside 37 Wiley Bottom Road.

As they ate buttered English muffins and traded sections of *The New York Times,* Lee waited for her mother to be distracted enough to give her time to search for the pills. Or maybe she would wait until Charlotte went to Publix for groceries. "Mom," she said, "I think we're out of sliced turkey."

"Nope, I got some!"

"Are we good for coffee and wine?"

"I think so," said Charlotte. Her eyes lifted from the paper and settled on Lee. Lee could tell Charlotte was wary.

"Great!" said Lee.

The wall phone rang and rang. Charlotte did the crossword puzzle with a felt-tip pen. Lee read a profile of scammer Anna Delvey in the Style section, then a story about looted Greek artifacts being held at the National Gallery in London. What was the deal with looters and scammers? Did no one have a moral compass anymore? Lee wasn't made for this world. Yet another reason, thought Lee, to exit.

Lee had been told by many mental health professionals over the years that Depression was telling her lies and she had to focus on reality. But what if Depression's proclamations and reality were one and the same?

"When the voice of depression drowns out your true heart's voice," one therapist had said, "that's when you are in danger."

Francine sent a text: did you post a TikTok about bikini?

Lee's true heart said, "I'm done."

The wall phone rang. Charlotte, dressed for tennis though no one was playing tennis, stood up. "Don't answer it!" said Lee.

"Honey," said Charlotte. "It could be someone from my golf

group. It could be an old friend who doesn't have my cellphone number."

"You know it's creditors."

"I suppose you're right," said Charlotte.

"Or maybe scammers," said Lee.

Charlotte raised one shoulder coquettishly and picked up the phone. "Hello?" she said. Her face went from anticipatory to concerned. "What?" she said. "Flora, what?"

Lee, hypervigilant (as always) slammed her coffee cup into its saucer. Flora was Lee's niece, her sister Regan's sixteen-year-old daughter.

"OK, OK," said Charlotte, into the receiver. "Honey, I'm sure your mom's fine. She went to her artsy thing, right? Her 'Momcation'? I understand, dear, but it's only . . . yes, yes, OK. Maybe she's not texting you because she just needs . . . sorry, Flora, what? What is a Find My phone? You've lost me, dear. Flora, have you called your father? Hm, well, OK. I don't blame you."

"What is it?" said Lee.

Charlotte nodded. "Mmhmm . . . OK . . . I truly don't think you need to worry, sweetheart. I truly don't. Listen. Flora. Flora, dear, calm down. Why don't you and your sister just go ahead and make yourselves a yummy, yummy dinner. Do you want me to email some recipes? There's a cashew chicken with broccoli from *The New York Times* . . . oh, OK, dear. Pizza sounds yummy, too!"

"Regan's missing?" said Lee.

Charlotte put her hand over the phone. "Pipe down!" she hissed at Lee.

"Sorry."

"I love you, Flora. OK, dear. I'll talk to you later, OK? Bye, now, honey. You enjoy your yummy, yummy pizza."

Charlotte replaced the phone, put her hand on the counter, and dropped her head, as if she were dizzy or had lost her balance. Then she straightened, put her shoulders back, and began to perform her favorite role, "Charlotte-without-a-care." (It was no mystery where Lee's performative talent had come from.)

"What is it?" asked Lee. "What happened?"

"Well," said Charlotte, sitting back down and sipping her coffee, "Regan went on a little . . ." Charlotte waved her hand in a circular motion. "A little 'Mom-cation.'"

"What does that mean?" said Lee.

"That's what they're calling it now, a Mom-cation. Anyway, she went to a scrapbooking event or some such. What could be more dull . . . but anyhoo. She left the girls to fend for themselves. I didn't like her plan, but whoever listens to little old me?"

"Why did Flora call?" said Lee, impatiently.

"Flora's a nervous Nelly. She just is. I'm sure everything's fine."

"But . . ." said Lee.

"I do hate them being so far away," admitted Charlotte. "Remember when they lived on She Crab Circle? Six minutes by golf cart! Now the girls don't have *anyone*."

"Yeah," said Lee. This thought made her sad.

Charlotte sighed. "Why did she go all the way to Greece, Lee Lee?"

"Because of her Vision Board Workshop," said Lee.

"Greece is so far away," said Charlotte, looking old.

All this sadness, and nothing you can do about it, said Depression.

Lee went to her mother and hugged her.

8 LEE

CHARLOTTE EMERGED FROM THE DEPTHS OF HER ATTIC CRAWL space, brushing dust from her hair. She held a large pink duffel bag in her hand. "I thought I had a suitcase in here," said Charlotte. "But there's no suitcase. I did find this monogrammed bag from L.L.Bean!"

"That's going to be heavy for you, Mom," said Lee.

"Oh, pish!" said Charlotte.

Pish? Lee swallowed her annoyance. She tightened the sash of the paisley-print bathrobe she'd borrowed from Charlotte, then sat on the floor outside the crawl space, sipping coffee. "What did Flora say, exactly?"

"Regan said she'd be home Sunday, but Flora's convinced Regan is in danger because . . . something about finding her phone," said Charlotte, continuing to rummage through mountains of holiday decorations. "Or maybe it's *not* finding her phone? I didn't really understand the nitty-gritty. But Flora is very worried and honestly, I can't stand it that they're all alone over there!" Charlotte sighed. "She's like you," she added.

"What does that mean?"

"Just that Flora worries more than she needs to."

"Oh," said Lee.

"I'm sure that's a hard way to be," said Charlotte. Lee was surprised and touched that her mother was acknowledging an uncomfortable subject.

"Yeah, it is," said Lee.

It *was* a hard way to be.

Charlotte proclaimed, "I never worry!"

"I know, Mom," said Lee, not noting that perhaps this was why Lee had been forced to handle all their family's worries from a young age.

"I just have fun!" proclaimed Charlotte. Then she whirled back around and continued her search for luggage. She said, "Regan will probably get back to Athens before I even land, but I can't just sit here and do nothing like an old lady!"

"Wait, Mom, you're going to Greece?" said Lee.

"Poor Flora. She's been taking a Greek subway to school. A subway! Honestly! Now it's nighttime over there and the girls are all alone in the dark. Flora said they don't have any adults to call. This is the problem with leaving your family!"

"Mom . . ." said Lee, standing up and approaching Charlotte.

"If you want to be helpful, buy me a plane ticket. To Greece. I suppose I'll need a rental car. I don't know! And who is going to watch you and all your sleeping pills? Honestly!"

Lee exhaled through her nose. "Let's just wait until Sunday and see if Regan comes home," she said, trying to sound reasonable.

"They're all alone in the dark!" said Charlotte.

"I'll go," said Lee. She was testing the words, but even as she spoke them, something familiar stirred in her chest. How many family calamities had she handled over the course of her childhood? How many times had she been the one to step in when everything fell apart?

Charlotte's relief was immediate and visible. Lee watched her mother's shoulders ease. And there it was again—that old, sick satisfaction of being needed. Even now, even when she wanted nothing more than to disappear, her family's crisis called to her like a drug.

A new plan emerged: Lee would go to Greece, fix whatever mess Regan had gotten into, and then fly back in first class. She'd sip champagne, wash down thirty pills . . . and savor absolute peace above the clouds. But first, she'd do what she'd always done: Save everyone else.

"Really? You'll go?" The hopefulness in her mother's voice made Lee realize how scared Charlotte had been at the thought of leaving home. This was another sadness—her mother had once been a jetsetter.

Charlotte had even fallen in love with a man named Paros during their family Mediterranean cruise. What had happened to Charlotte's romance with Paros? Lee had never even asked.

"Maybe we should both go to Greece," said Charlotte. "They told me to keep very close watch on your pills. . . ."

"Just the sleeping pills, Mom," Lee clarified. "I can handle the rest myself."

"Those are the ones I'm worried about," Charlotte replied.

"Really, Mom," said Lee. "I'll be fine."

There's one way to be finally, finally fine, said Depression.

Charlotte narrowed her eyes and looked at her eldest daughter. Lee arranged her face to convey contentment and competence, meeting her mother's gaze directly, raising the corners of her mouth into a relaxed (but not creepy) smile, tilting her head encouragingly. Her favorite acting coach had been a devotee of Stella Adler's "imaginative detachment," which instructed that "the actor must not use his own life to create a role; he must use the life of the character." Lee tried to become a person who had their shit together, to convey this energy to Charlotte.

Charlotte, hoodwinked—or simply worn-out—nodded, smiling. "OK," she said. "I do have golf on Friday," she added.

"How old are Flora and Isabelle again?" said Lee. Now that her plan was set, she actually did feel anticipation, an emotion that had eluded her for a long time. This lightness was common with depressives who'd made an exit strategy, she knew. It felt good.

"Isabelle is eighteen," said Charlotte. "And Flora just had her sixteenth birthday party. Regan took them to a mall. A mall! In Athens, Greece! They couldn't even read the Greek alphabet to find a place for manicures. How depressing. Anyhoo, do you want this monogrammed duffel bag, Lee?"

"No thanks, Mom."

"Suit yourself," said Charlotte, dropping the duffel and climbing out of the crawl space. "Now, did you also say you'd call Matt?"

"Ugh," said Lee. She hadn't spoken to her sister's ex-husband since the divorce. Lee had seen him at Palmetto Pool with his young, pregnant wife, but she had avoided them. Once, Lee and Matt had been hot-and-heavy high school sweethearts. Then Lee had dumped Matt and moved to California. Matt had married Regan and treated her badly. The thought of speaking to smug old Mansplaining Matt made Lee feel queasy.

"Let me get the plane ticket," said Lee.

"I'll finish the crossword," said Charlotte.

Lee had once had a personal assistant named Val. Lee texted her, and Val agreed to look at airfares even though she was now employed by a Real Housewife of Orange County. (Val, who had a septum piercing, was not loving Orange County.)

"Mom," said Lee, following Charlotte into the kitchen. "Whatever happened to Paros?"

Charlotte dropped her felt-tip pen. Otherwise, she did not react. After a few seconds, she picked up her pen again. "Who?" she said.

"Paros? The Greek man from our cruise?"

"Oh, *Paros,*" said Charlotte. "Hm . . . I honestly have no idea."

Lee heard the words even without Charlotte speaking: *and furthermore.* This was Charlotte's shorthand for "this conversation is over."

Lee's phone chimed and she let the moment go. "Val can get me to Houston tonight," said Lee. "And to Athens in the morning."

"Good," said Charlotte. "Let's call the girls."

When was the last time Lee had spoken to her nieces? She'd once gazed at her sister's social media photos longingly, perhaps obsessively. But Lee's stardom had enabled her to begrudgingly accept her spinsterhood. Unfortunately, the Covid shutdown and tedium of life with her mother had reignited an ember of regret in her gut, and she'd begun peeking at Regan's posts of her teen-aged daughters again: Flora at the Acropolis, both girls eating gyros, Isabelle wearing sunglasses and holding a frappé iced cof-fee. Sixteen-year-old Flora wore round glasses, parted her blond hair in the middle, and seemed willing enough to have her picture taken. Isabelle was an eighteen-year-old with one or more tat-toos, her expression often challenging.

When Lee was eighteen, she'd already been taking care of her siblings and her own mother for years. Some eighteen-year-olds had kids of their own! Yet Lee had to begrudgingly admit it felt good to be needed.

As Charlotte dialed her granddaughters, Lee felt weirdly shy. "Isabelle, sweetheart," said Charlotte. "Your Auntie Lee is going to come visit. Can you feed your sister for one more night? I'm sure your mom will come home while Auntie Lee is en route, but Flora seems worried . . . do you want to talk to Auntie Lee? What? Oh, that's fine, dear. I'll tell her."

Charlotte hung up the phone, turning to Lee with an overly cheerful smile.

"She didn't want to talk to me?" said Lee, stung. Her nieces, especially Flora, held themselves at a distance from their aunt. They were polite but aloof at family gatherings, hiding behind books or their devices when Lee tried to engage them. Did they think she was pathetic? Lee felt wobbly. She'd secretly hoped that her nieces thought she was amazing for being a reality TV star. But maybe teenagers thought reality TV was embarrassing.

It was also possible that her nieces didn't think about Lee at all.

"Oh, who knows," said Charlotte. "Don't be dramatic. Did you buy your ticket?"

"Do you think Regan's hurt . . . or kidnapped or something?" said Lee, deftly turning her self-hatred into concern for her sister. In the psychiatric hospital, Lee was told that her messy childhood had left her with complex PTSD. Her therapist had said it was as if she had actual scars, and certain events could open the wounds, sending her brain back in time. Her biggest trigger, apparently, was when her younger siblings or mother needed her. Watching Charlotte put her hand to her mouth made Lee feel responsible, as she'd felt after her father's suicide. *Someone needs to handle this, whatever this is,* her heart said. *And that someone is going to be you.*

It was the oldest pattern in her playbook—crisis hits, Lee steps up, Lee fixes things, everyone else gets to fall apart safely. She was addicted, they told her in group, to "emotional intoxication," and had to fight her urge to visit "the emotional drugstore." Lee couldn't remember what the "drugstore" was in this metaphor. Was her missing sister the "drugstore"?

"You pack," said Charlotte. "And I'll bring you up some peanut butter crackers."

As Lee filled her suitcase, Charlotte appeared in the doorway holding a small pharmacy bottle. "Here," she said, extending it toward Lee with obvious reluctance.

Lee looked at the bottle—seven white pills rattled inside. "A week's worth?"

"That should be plenty," Charlotte said. "You'll find your sister and be back before you know it."

Lee pocketed the medication, feeling the familiar weight of Charlotte's worry. "Thanks, Mom. I'll be fine."

Charlotte nodded, unconvinced but out of options. "Promise me you won't—"

"Of course, Mom. I promise."

Both Lee and her mother knew that promises about depression were impossible to keep.

9 LEE

AS LEE'S PLANE DESCENDED INTO ATHENS INTERNATIONAL AIRPORT, she watched shadows of sprawling islands taking shape below, framed by glimmering cobalt water. Each Greek island was distinct: one mountainous, another densely populated on one side. Lee's gaze swept across olive groves and whitewashed buildings, temples, small harbors, and sandy beaches. The aircraft approached the mainland. Lee tried—and failed—to remember her high school lessons about Greek gods and goddesses.

Athens was a sprawling cityscape of low-rise buildings with flat roofs. Lee saw the honey-colored marble walls and columns of the Acropolis. Roads originating at the ancient city center formed a web of threads that led toward modern neighborhoods. Jagged mountain peaks surrounded the capital, a mixture of rocky and forested terrain.

How had it been ten years since Lee and her family had boarded the *Splendido Marveloso* cruise ship in Greece? Lee rummaged in her purse for the peanut butter crackers Charlotte had pressed into her hand at the Savannah airport the day before. Lee had refused the moist packet, but Charlotte said, "Trust me, Lee Lee—you'll want peanut butter crackers eventually."

As always—and infuriatingly—Charlotte was right.

"Get a ginger ale to go with," Charlotte had advised. "Or an airplane cup of chardonnay!"

Lee ripped the plastic package open with her teeth and stared out of the window, jamming a gritty, greasy cracker in her mouth. The plane jostled, and Lee grabbed the armrest. Her mind raced back to the last time she had spoken to Regan. Lee had been embarrassed about her breakdown; she'd avoided answering calls from her siblings. When the sisters finally spoke, Lee had kept the conversation brief. Regan had mentioned a new boyfriend, a "math guy" named François.

"Is he French? Where did you meet?" said Lee.

"Oh, well . . ." said Regan, with a weak little giggle.

After a moment, during which Lee had been scrolling on her phone, Lee snapped to attention. "Oh, well, *what*?" she said.

"Well, we met online, if you must know," said Regan, so defensively that Lee felt a flare of concern.

"Like . . . on a dating app?" asked Lee suspiciously.

"Oh my God, no," twittered Regan. "On Facebook! Anyway, I've got to run. You'll meet him! He's real, I promise. And yes, he's French!"

Lee's plane touched down, decelerating on the runway. Her seatbelt pinched her waist, and there was a dull thudding behind her eyeballs. She chewed her last peanut butter cracker. When there was a ding, passengers all around Lee jumped to their feet to grab their overstuffed suitcases. Lee peered out at a rainy, gray day.

Of course, it was entirely possible that Regan was safe and might return home any minute. She might be in her Athens apartment already! But Lee felt uneasy. She would know if Regan were dead, wouldn't she?

And who found romance on Facebook? It definitely seemed sketchy. But if François was not a fabulous new boyfriend, who was he—and what had he done?

10 REGAN & FRANÇOIS

ONE YEAR EARLIER

TOWARD THE END OF THE PANDEMIC, IT HAD SEEMED LIKE SUCH A great idea for Regan to triple-mask, face-shield, and haul her girls out of the country. Her ex-husband, Matt, the girls' father, had gotten his new girlfriend pregnant, and as soon as Regan heard the news (from one of her school mom friends—not even from Matt himself!), she vowed that her daughters would never see that baby. How could she keep them from their half brother or sister? She could become an expat, that's how, but where?

She'd signed up for a Vision Board Workshop at a nearby yoga studio. Along with a group, Regan had dutifully cut out magazine photos. "Just cut out the images that call to you," encouraged the instructor.

This process was similar to the art Regan had been constructing for years—she'd called it "collage" as a young student and "scrapbooking" as a wife. Regan rescued what others saw as detritus: She always had. Charlotte had once despaired of Regan's pockets full of littered receipts, dirty coins, used lotto tickets. But Regan would sit for entire afternoons arranging the trash and her own drawings, creating what she believed was art.

Regan stopped, rewound, and edited herself—*creating art*. Full stop. Why was it difficult to see herself as someone whose work—whose life—had value?

At the end of the workshop, Regan's board was covered with photos of the Acropolis; the Greek Islands; a person painting; a fierce woman looking out an airplane window; and various handcrafted ceramics. She saw then that it was time to shed her downtrodden divorcée persona, get up off the yoga studio floor, and flee the country. She'd done the toddler years and put up with a bad man in her life for long enough. It was Regan's time to shine.

That night, Regan googled "best places artist sexy." The divorce agreement had given Regan her large Savannah home and monthly alimony. The house was worth a million dollars. Wearing her #1 MOM sweatshirt and sipping a vodka–Diet Coke, she scrolled the list of possible lives:

NUMBER ONE: Paris. Regan opened a tab and read, deciding it was too expensive and also, French women seemed off-putting and frighteningly suave.

NUMBER TWO: New York. Nope, nope, nope: not far enough from Matt and his Baby Momma, a young woman who had once been the girls' teacher at Savannah Country Day.

NUMBER THREE: Mexico City. Regan paused, but nah. She'd never been to Mexico. It seemed overwhelming and she liked Mexican food a bit too much.

She had reservations, too, about numbers four and five, Berlin and Kyoto.

But number six was Athens, Greece.

Athens, Greece! The city where her weird and wonderful family vacation had begun, a ten-day cruise from Athens to Barcelona. It was the trip that had ruined her life in the perfect way. Regan could envision herself striding past the Acropolis. In her imagination, she wore a cape of some sort with knee-high boots. One more Google search—"Zillow apartments for sale Acropolis Athens Greece"—and she was on her way. Regan called a realtor friend and sold her She Crab Circle property in a week.

While packing up her adult life, Regan allowed herself to keep photos, notes, and clippings of any kind that she could work into collages. She took breaks to peruse Facebook, where she followed artists she admired—visual artists mostly, many of whom worked in collage, but also some painters, ceramicists, and installation artists. She peeked into these strangers' workshops with envy, commented on their new work, and then somehow ended up in the section called People You May Know.

One of the people she might know was named François. Such a sexy name, thought Regan, who had not had a boyfriend since her divorce, despite the school moms encouraging her to "get on the apps."

In the People You May Know section of Facebook, Regan clicked on François's profile picture. He was a handsome man with a white mustache and a crinkly cheeked smile. François was a mathematician at Institut des Hautes Études Scientifiques, south of Paris. Regan knew he might not be real, but she also knew he *might* be real. Why was François a person she might know? How did Facebook connect Regan and a handsome mathematician in France? Kismet, she decided, and requested his friendship. It all seemed innocent: *Click!*

A *bloop* sound alerted her to a note in Facebook Messenger— a note from François:

It read, Hello.

Hello, Regan responded.

How are you today?

In a departure, Regan was honest: Honestly, a little lonely.

I am also a little lonely. Are you at work?

Regan paused. At this point, packing and envisioning a new future was—in fact—her work. She typed, Yes.

You have a beautiful smile, wrote François.

Regan stared at the screen, rereading the words. *Beautiful.* No one ever called Regan beautiful. She was always "the good one," the "younger sister of Lee Perkins," praised for her subservience and kindheartedness, her cooking and mothering.

But to this stranger, Regan wasn't Lee's pudgy little sister or Matt's disappointing wife. She *had a beautiful smile.* Regan scrutinized her profile picture, which had been taken at a wedding long ago. Not her wedding. She wore a pink silk top and matching lipstick.

Thank you, wrote Regan. She felt warm.

Regan remembered the first time a man had really seen her—it had been her high school art teacher, Mr. Ragdale. He had been leaning against his blackboard, wearing khaki pants with his shirt tucked in. Regan walked by, and when she turned around he was watching her and his face was soft as if she were special.

Regan had felt warm then, too.

11 CHARLOTTE

CHARLOTTE'S CAT, GODIVA, HAD PASSED AWAY, AND SHE WAS JUST too old to get a new kitten. Once in a while, Charlotte saw an aged animal (like herself!) on the Savannah Humane Society adoption page, but honestly, what could be more depressing? Still, she missed having something to feed, cuddle, and let in and out of her kitchen sliding door.

With Lee on a flight to Greece, Charlotte meandered around her house, nibbling cheese and crackers and opening and closing the little drawers of her antique side tables. In one drawer, she found her first love letter from Paros, which he had placed on her room service breakfast tray on the morning the *Splendido Marveloso* docked in Sicily, Italy. The paper was thin and crinkled; it read:

> *Homer wrote in the Odyssey that a many headed monster (SCYLLA) guarded the entrance to the Strait of Messina and ate sailors who tried to approach . . . and that the whirlpool CHA-RYBDIS waited for vessels . . . Luckily, the Splendido Marveloso has already safely docked. I love the view of Sicily and the Ca-labrian coast and I hope you have a wonderful day.*
>
> *Yours,*
> *Paros*

Charlotte stared at the letter. It was an odd note, truth be told. Did Paros write notes to all the single ladies aboard his ships? Perhaps he'd found someone new by now.

Perhaps he was dead.

Charlotte went to her garage to grab a fresh bottle of Barefoot Chardonnay from the wine refrigerator. She looked at her new golf cart, her old car. For a moment, she thought of Minnie, her best friend, who had died over a decade before.

Charlotte wrenched her mind away from Minnie—how devastating her sudden death had been! There was absolutely *no point* in thinking about sad and worrisome things. Sometimes, to keep herself cheerful—to avoid worrying about Lee and her sleeping pills, for example, to trust her daughter when Lee said she was "fine" even though Charlotte's gut told her otherwise—Charlotte needed wine. She twisted her corkscrew feverishly, pulled the cork, filled her glass.

And furthermore.

It was a lonely thing, growing elderly. Becoming a "senior." You thought you were old at seventy, but that had nothing on your eighties. A man at church—Bruce Lark—had started saying, "Half my friends are dead, and the other half are half-dead!" He said it every Sunday after mass when they drank coffee and ate Publix pastries. It had been funny the first time Charlotte heard it, but after that, not so much.

Anyhoo! Charlotte drank deeply, topped off her wine, went to her living room, and turned on her electric fireplace and her television. Turner Classic Movies was showing *The Wizard of Oz*. That was exciting.

12 LEE

REGAN HAD TOLD LEE THEY CALLED HER NEW NEIGHBORHOOD, Plaka, "The Neighborhood of the Gods," but Lee was skeptical. From the window of her taxi, Lee observed the crowded avenues surrounding the Acropolis. Horns blared and motorbikes scarcely missed knocking down throngs of tourists and street performers like one hapless fellow juggling flaming torches (why?). Actual antiquities were surrounded by modern buildings with bougainvillea-draped terraces, an appealing café here and there among the tables of crap for sale. (Though Lee noted that one guy was hawking some cute leather sandals.) Lee's driver stopped at the end of a precariously narrow cobblestone street. "Can't go farther," he said, followed by the "yess-us" word that must mean "get out of my taxi."

"Why not?" said Lee.

"Pedestrian only," said the driver, pointing to a blue sign that read, incomprehensibly to Lee: Μόνο Πεζοί.

The driver added, "Mono-pe-zee," and lit a cigarette.

"Jesus H. Christ," said Lee. She hauled her bags out of the car with no help from the driver, who watched her struggle as he smoked, his elbow on his open windowsill. Two wheelie bags behind her and a purse hanging across her chest, Lee hobbled down

Regan's street, Dionysiou Aeropagitou. She located her sister's address, a weathered but charming building.

In the front garden, a sleek cat lounged in a patch of sunlight between terra-cotta planters overflowing with jasmine. On a second-story balcony, two teenagers stared at their phones. Lee swallowed as it dawned on her that the teenagers were her nieces. "Isabelle? Flora?" called Lee.

They looked up from their glowing devices. Isabelle wore a crop top that was way too cropped, bare feet, and loose pajama pants that belonged to her mother—Lee recognized them from a Christmas long ago when Charlotte had given her adult children matching pajamas. Her hair was parted in the middle like Marcia in that old TV show *The Brady Bunch*. Lee saw herself in Isabelle's calculated dishevelment—the way she held her shoulders back a bit, the tilt of her chin that said, *I know I'm beautiful and I know you're looking.*

Sixteen-year-old Flora was pudgy, as her mom had been. Her too-small shorts cut into her thighs, and she wore Doc Martens boots. Both girls gazed at Lee vacantly, and Lee felt the familiar sting of the girls' careful remove, the way her younger niece, especially, always seemed to be bracing herself whenever Lee appeared. What was it about Lee that made Flora reticent? Lee flushed with middle school vulnerability: *Why don't they like me?*

"Girls," said Lee. Their wary expressions cracked, and they rushed down the stairs to Lee, claiming her with powerful hugs.

"Mom's still not home," whispered Isabelle. "Flora's really scared."

These poor pandemic children, thought Lee. *Thank God I'm here to rescue them.*

13 LEE

LEE AND THE GIRLS BROUGHT HER LUGGAGE UPSTAIRS. ISABELLE fumbled with keys to three different locks and shoved open the door. As Lee stepped inside, she was struck by the appealing apartment.

How was it possible that in this unknown city, Regan had made a home that smelled so similar to her old house in Savannah? A fragrance that was difficult to parse, combining Regan's strawberry shampoo, Lubriderm lotion, vanilla candles, and the glue sticks she used in her collages. Her chicken noodle soup and the mac and cheese she made with spaghetti and way, way too much cheddar. The scent was Regan herself: homey and loving.

And Lee's little sister had taken such care in designing this space! In the center of the living room was a mid-century modern couch newly upholstered in a mint-green fabric and a dinged-up-but-recently-polished coffee table. Two mismatched end tables held lamps with new shades. A large desk in the corner of the room was a neatly organized workstation for Regan's collage art—there were the glue sticks, X-Acto knives, scissors, tape in various colors, and a row of flat boxes that must have held works in progress. A small radio anchored a pile of clippings.

The walls were wood-paneled, very "late-eighties party basement." Above the couch, Lee saw a giant, bad painting of the Acropolis in a rococo frame. In the corner was a signature: *Dennis Royale.*

Around the painting, Regan had hung her own creations. Lee walked over to peer at one collage, which featured an old Willingham Christmas card. Both Regan and Matt had been excised from the card, leaving Isabelle and Flora in the center, smiling stiltedly. Regan had surrounded her girls with images of birds and waves, and covered the Christmas tree with cutouts of pink-and-purple blossoms, leaving the impression of unmoored children surrounded by fragile flowers—a jarring image, but piercingly beautiful and somehow suffused with hope. Lee was heartened that Regan had returned to her art—she was really talented.

The coffee table was covered with art and photography books—*Collage: The Making of Modern Art; Collage by Women: 50 Essential Contemporary Artists; Greece: History and Treasures of an Ancient Civilization;* and *Aegean: The Invention of the Sea.*

Lee recognized a framed poster of a painting that had once hung in Regan's teenaged bedroom: Degas's *The Star.* Lee stared at the ballerina in the image, a young girl in a pale tutu, her arms extended gracefully, eyes lifted toward the spotlight. Lee remembered lying on Regan's carpeted bedroom floor, reading or pretending to read as their father's drunken voice thundered below them. Regan and Cord would snuggle in Regan's bed, Lee hoping that her presence made them feel safe, or at least safer. Teenaged Lee would stare at Degas's ballerina and wish for her siblings the vulnerability and radiance on the dancer's face. With Lee as constant sentinel, she hoped her brother and sister, at least, could have a childhood.

Flora and Isabelle looked at her expectantly. The fog of despair that had enveloped Lee in Savannah thinned—just a tiny bit—as Lee felt that old tug: the need to fix, to be the watchman.

She put her hands on her hips. She had not flown all night to wallow in childhood memories.

"Tell me everything," she said, sitting in a caramel-colored chair. "From the beginning."

Lee noticed Flora's careful posture, the way she sat with her hands folded, waiting for permission to speak. It was very different from the chatty, enthusiastic child Flora had been before Lee's first hospitalization. "You can relax, Flora," Lee said gently.

Flora's eyes widened slightly. Nervously, she said, "Mom went to a collage retreat on Santorini on Tuesday. She left this." As Lee looked over Regan's note, Flora continued, "But she didn't text me back that night, and when I checked Find My, her phone was disabled!"

"There's no way Mom disabled Find My on her own," noted Isabelle.

"And I searched for the Santorini retreat online. It doesn't exist," said Flora.

"The truth is, Mom's been different for months," said Isabelle, quietly.

"Different how?" Lee leaned forward.

"She started renting out one of our rooms on Airbnb. She said we'd be able to afford NYU, my dream school, even though we're broke. And she . . . she spends all day on her computer, like, texting with her boyfriend, François."

"She's never seen him in person," added Flora. "Not even on a video chat."

The pieces clicked into place with sickening clarity. Lee had seen enough *Dateline* episodes to know where this was heading.

"Flora," Lee said carefully, "you mentioned you know about online scams?"

"I'm doing a school report about *pig butchering*," said Flora.

"They make you fall in love, then steal your money. And Mom's been acting exactly like the victims I've been researching."

"Mom's not stupid, though," said Isabelle.

Flora looked at her boots. "Smart people get scammed too. That's what makes it work."

Lee wanted to calm the girls, assure them their mother was safe. She also knew she needed to protect what was left of her own fragile mental health. Instead, she heard herself say, "You're right. We need to find your mom *now*."

The girls looked at their aunt, alarmed, and Lee realized they'd assumed Lee would placate them and offer hope. Lee felt an old weight settle on her shoulders—the responsibility of being in charge. But this time, it wasn't just family drama. This was real danger. Lee knew she had no choice. "We need to find her now," Lee repeated. "Let's get to work."

14 REGAN & FRANÇOIS

THE THRILL OF BITCOIN INVESTING WAS EVEN BETTER THAN DRINK-
ing three skinny margaritas at Jalapeño's, Regan's favorite restaurant in Savannah. After months of François boasting about all the
money he was making on the side—sending her photos of expensive handbags and asking her to help pick out one for his mother;
asking Regan whether he should order the turbot or blue lob-
ster medallions at the three-Michelin-star restaurant Le Cinq—
he finally relented and told Regan he'd teach her how to make
some money, too. Via text (they never spoke or video-chatted), he
walked her through using something called Tether to transform
three hundred dollars from her checking account into Bitcoin,
sending her screenshots to help.

When Regan opened an account on Kraken Futures, an online trading platform, François wrote: I'm proud of you. There is
nothing sexier than an independent woman.

Don't get too excited! Regan responded, though it did give
her a thrill to see three hundred dollars of Bitcoin in her Tether
wallet.

I love a sugar mama, joked François. I've never liked Matt controlling you.

Regan frowned. It was true that Matt handled their investments, dismissing her questions and telling her to focus on being a mother. But François explained everything so clearly in his messages, treating Regan as if she were as smart as he, an equal. He wrote about museum exhibits he visited on the weekend; he taught her how the algorithms he created were able to trade on the millisecond. François was fascinated by Regan's desire to create art. He told her about a book by the producer of the Beastie Boys' music called *The Creative Act*. A copy arrived, sent from a local English-language bookshop, and Regan and François read chapters together, François asking Regan about her collage art, encouraging her to visit Athenian exhibits and report back. No one had ever respected Regan's mind before; it was wholly intoxicating.

Regan's heart raced as François showed her how to place her first trade, a "time to trade" bet on Bitcoin movement. François gave her inside intel from another math wonk at his job, and Regan placed the bet.

She made a cup of tea in her kitchen to have something to do while she waited. Outside her kitchen window, she could glimpse the Acropolis, which still seemed like an impossible miracle. But she had pulled it off.

In fifteen minutes, Regan was up $160.

How do you feel? wrote François.

Amazing! Is this what gambling feels like?

This is skilled trading, Regan. Gambling is for fools. You have natural talent.

François conveyed how to transfer the money back to her bank account. All night, as she cooked, cleaned, did laundry, folded clothes, she checked her bank app. The profit was still there. Real money. Her money. Not Matt's.

LOVE HACKERS
BY FLORA WILLINGHAM

For my First Year Lyceum, I decided to complete a multidisciplinary research project about the romance scam industry and title my project "Love Hackers," which is one of the things the scammers call themselves in their online forums.

WHY I CHOSE THIS SUBJECT

I first became aware of romance scammers, or "pig butcherers," when my mother was victimized. She was smart, self-sufficient, and loved me and my sister. How and why did she believe the lies of a romance scammer? And who and where was the person who stole her away?

HOW DO ROMANCE SCAMS WORK?

For my **literature research** component, I am including a training manual for "pig butchering" that I found on a Chinese website. Pig butchering is the term for a scam where a predator builds trust with a victim, often through a fake romantic relationship, and then they manipulate the victim into investing large sums of money in fake schemes, typically involving cryptocurrency—the term refers to "fattening up the pig" before "slaughtering" them by taking their money.

I ordered a translation of the Chinese manual, and learned that scammers are taught "packaging must be realistic." Your name, says the manual, should not be "crude," though you can have a "nickname naughty and cute." A fake persona's age should be between 28 and 35: "Cannot be too young (childish without experience) or too old (unattractive)." As you craft your fake identity's geographical location, the manual advises, "understand the tastes, snacks, scenic spots, main streets, ethnic customs, celebrities, etc."

As for your photo, choose an image that is "mature, handsome, muscles, use full-length photos as profile pics, make very clear, if possible with short videos. Can use customers of other co-workers. If using [other] customers' photos, find the ones that meet the above conditions for packaging!"

Recommended family backgrounds include "born in military, government official, teacher, artist, with good education and family upbringing, values and understanding."

Here are some more excerpts from the manual that I found disturbing:

GRASPING THE CUSTOMER'S PSYCHOLOGY
- Arouse the customer's inner dreams, goals, bring out a fighting state of mind (motivation)
- Create dreams of perfection, allow customers to fantasize living better and living in their dream life (enjoyment)

HOW TO SET THE HOOK
- Send two pictures of luxury bags or jewelry to the guest and ask the guest to help choose one, hinting to the guest that one has recently made a considerable amount of extra income and wants to buy a gift for customer.
- Send photos of high-end restaurants and comment on their expensive and palatable meals. Better off to stabilize the side

income first, or it's too wasteful. You can ask the guest what
they usually do when they are bored. After the guest answers,
they will usually ask you what you have done and you will have a
chance to get in.
- You can say: travel, walking the streets/window shopping,
  listening to music, playing mahjong, making money with Bitcoin
  investments.

My mom never actually video-chatted with her so-called boyfriend.
I freaked out a bit when I read this in the "Pig Butchering Manual":

How to avoid meeting on video chats: (Do not disclose in the early
days! When the relationship is deep, capitalize on this to avoid
video chats.) Tell the story of a very sad, strict upbringing, also
autism/other psychological conditions. When the customer uses
feelings to pressure you to meet by video chat, disclose a fear that
this side of you (childhood and/or autistic distress of cameras)
might show up again. The female customer's natural maternal
love will instinctively come out and they will no longer pressure
you.

    If you cannot avoid, consult a Video Editor for help.

16 LEE

AFTER DINNER—MCDONALD'S BURGERS DELIVERED BY A GREEK ON a moped—Lee moved into Regan's room and began looking through her sister's things. Regan's phone was missing, her car was missing, Regan was missing, and her laptop was missing.

Lee hadn't really paid much attention to her sister for a long time. She'd assumed Regan as a mother and adult was who she'd been as a kid: the one you didn't have to worry about. When Regan and Matt divorced and Regan moved to Greece, Lee had been jealous, but never concerned. Now she felt guilty for not noticing her sister had been in trouble, but also weirdly glad to have a purpose to tie her to the world for a bit. The only time Lee glimpsed happiness seemed to be when she was enmeshed, or codependent, or whatever you wanted to call it. When she was needed.

Regan's bedroom had three Japanese fans affixed to the wall (why?). Her bed was lumpy but the sheets seemed clean. In the bathroom, Lee looked at her sister's toiletries. When she had been a doctor's wife, Regan had used "Purple" shampoo to keep her blond highlights gleaming. She'd ordered expensive skin care products, nicer than any Lee used and Lee's face was literally her job. But in her reimagined, Athenian life, Regan used cheap Suave

products. She had a large, almost empty bottle of off-brand vita-
mins for women. Her mirrored cabinet needed Windexing.

Lee ached. She'd imagined her sister's life in Greece was glamorous . . . a whitewashed beachside cottage, furniture made of rattan.
Instead, Regan's home was well loved but sparsely furnished, a
three-bedroom apartment with one room rented to strangers.

At least Regan still had her luxurious monogrammed towels
and bath mat. Lee's shoulders softened as she stepped under a
stream of hot water in Regan's shower. She exhaled and closed
her eyes. Lee's depression seemed distant—the need to find her
sister had snapped her back to herself.

Sunday morning, Lee would rise early (she'd need to set an
alarm!) and prepare breakfast for the girls (did they have English
muffins?). Then, if Regan did not return or text, Lee would call
the police.

Lee wasn't terrified, not yet. Regan had obviously gotten into
some sort of scrape, but lurid crimes seemed like something that
happened to other families. The Perkinses had had enough trauma
to last them, and it seemed impossible that Regan had been ran-
domly abducted or sold into sex trafficking. Who would abduct a
mom?

Changing into pajamas, Lee opened the drawer of her sister's
nightstand: ChapStick, an unopened Kiss chocolate bar, a claw
clip, three hairbands, CBD lotion, an eye mask, earplugs, measur-
ing tape, cough drops, Sibley Backyard Birding flash cards. While
the private investigator part of herself had hoped to find a clue,
she was relieved that the contents of Regan's bedside drawer
were innocuous.

She made a last swipe of the drawer and her fingers closed on
a velvet box tucked into the back corner. Lee removed the box
and opened it, her heart beating fast.

The box was empty.

17 LEE

AFTER BREAKFAST ON SUNDAY, THE APARTMENT GREW ELECTRIC with waiting. Lee unpacked, pulling out her leopard-print toiletry case to check when her prescriptions would run out. She knew she needed to be careful to avoid returning to a state of "invisible agony," a description she'd found on page 696 of the novel *Infinite Jest* sent by her mental hospital pal, Remington. When Lee read the sentences, she had felt so deeply understood that she had ripped out the page and stashed it in her case:

> The so-called "psychotically depressed" person who tries to kill herself doesn't do so out of quote "hopelessness" or any abstract conviction that life's assets and debits do not square. And surely not because death seems suddenly appealing. The person in whom invisible agony reaches a certain unendurable level will kill herself the same way a trapped person will eventually jump from the window of a burning high-rise. Make no mistake about people who leap from burning windows. Their terror of falling from a great height is still just as great as it would be for you or me standing speculatively at the same window just checking out the view; i.e. the fear of falling remains a constant. The variable here is the other ter-

ror, the fire's flames: when the flames get close enough, falling to death becomes the slightly less terrible of two terrors. It's not desiring the fall; it's terror of the flames. And yet nobody down on the sidewalk, looking up and yelling "Don't!" and "Hang on!," can understand the jump. Not really. You'd have to have personally been trapped and felt flames to really understand a terror way beyond falling.

"A terror way beyond falling"—while mania was thrilling and powerful, David Foster Wallace's words described Lee's emotions *after mania* precisely. And her depressive thoughts never fully went away, not even when Lee did everything she was told.

Lee had plenty of her antidepressant, but when she shook the amber bottle of her mood stabilizer, her heart sank—only three pills left. She made a mental note to find a pharmacy as soon as possible. At least Charlotte had given her a week's worth of sleeping pills.

Regan said she would return *by lunchtime.* Lee heated canned soup and dumped it into bowls for the girls. She called them to the table and as they spooned the salty repast into their mouths, Lee asked insipid questions about their studies.

Regan did not come home.

Her phone was still disabled and not responding.

Isabelle confided that her mom had not let them watch *Breaking Bad.* Could they watch the violent show now, with their aunt? Jet-lagged Lee shrugged: She loved *Breaking Bad.* The three women huddled on the couch, watching *Breaking Bad* and watching the front door, which did not open.

At four P.M., Isabelle got dressed and went out, saying she was "meeting friends." When Lee asked when she would return, Isabelle said, "Who knows?"

Lee knew from all her teeny roles on police procedurals that it was important to get professionals involved ASAP in a missing persons case. She looked up the number for the Hellenic Police. Leaving Flora to watch a completely inappropriate meth-fueled sex scene, Lee stepped outside the apartment and dialed.

"Ελληνική Αστυνομία, πώς μπορώ να σας βοηθήσω?"

"Excuse me?" said Lee. She could not have been more confounded—the Greek language was so foreign she had no idea how many words had just been uttered, much less their possible meaning. "Do you speak English? My sister is missing."

"Moment, English," said the female voice.

"What?" said Lee.

"Tourist Police, call 1571," said the woman, sounding utterly bored, as if this may have been her hundredth missing persons call of the day.

"She is not a tourist!" said Lee. "She lives here! My sister lives in Athens with her teenaged daughters. She left for an artist retreat but she was supposed to come back today and she's not back."

"Do you believe your sister is in imminent danger?"

"She isn't answering her phone or responding to texts," said Lee. She did, in fact, think her sister could be in danger, but she also knew that her beliefs sometimes didn't align with reality.

"Have you checked the hospitals, jails, and mental health facilities in your surrounding area?"

"No . . ." said Lee.

"Have you located her phone and/or other devices? Laptop, iPad, tablet, desktop computer?"

"She took them with her, and she disabled Find My, the tracking app."

"Call us back if she's still missing in the morning. In the meantime, look into hospitals, jails, and mental health facilities. I hope your sister is returned," said the woman, followed by something that sounded like "yess-us" and also, at the same time, sounded like a cough.

"Thank you," said Lee. She sighed, remembering Regan, and how she used to curl up next to Lee as a kid and suck her thumb. Regan would scooch as close as possible to her big sister, facing away from her, lining her back up with Lee's shoulder and left side. Regan had been very warm. Cord, their brother, would sit on the other side of Regan and let her put her little feet in his lap.

Lee sent Val in Orange County a request to call the jails, mental health facilities, and hospitals in Athens. She said she'd pay whatever Val wanted and that Val might want a Greek-speaker on board to translate. Val was a genius at getting shit done, no matter how complicated.

Tell me anything you find, Lee wrote.

Val gave the message a thumbs-up.

Lee called her brother, Cord, to fill him in. He didn't answer, and Lee didn't leave a voicemail.

Lee had to stop being heartbroken every time Cord showed himself to be who he now was. Sure, he had once been the bright light of Lee's life—kind, earnest, devoted to his mom and sisters. It wasn't that Lee couldn't live without him—it was that it had never occurred to her she would have to. He'd been the glue who had held the Perkins family members together, and now he was not. They were on their own.

Still, she might try to call her little brother again tomorrow.

She missed his voice. She just did.

18 CORD

vanni, who had the time to record such things), Cord and Giovanni went to Panna II, the only restaurant left in what was once called Little India, on New York's Lower East Side. Where there had been four windows filled with flashing holiday lights, now there was Panna II surrounded by three dark and empty storefronts—another casualty of the pandemic.

"May our holiday lights continue to burn bright," said Giovanni, squeezing Cord's knee under the bright red tablecloth.

"I'm going to have a seizure," said Cord. Had the strings of multicolored bulbs always flashed erratically? Had they always hung so low? Many were burned-out, which seemed like a clear fire hazard and an even clearer metaphor. "I've never been here sober," Cord mused. "Honestly, I'm not sure I *want* to be here sober."

"Cord . . . it's been ten years since we got engaged," began Giovanni, before he was interrupted by a little boy—he must have been twelve. The kid wore a shiny three-piece suit and skinny tie.

"Welcome to Panna II, where Christmas happens all year

long!" he said in a practiced manner. "Can I interest you in mango lassis or have you brought your own wine?"

"I'll have Perrier in a glass," said Cord. He was pretending to be sober when outside their apartment.

"Same here," said Giovanni with a sigh.

"As a gentle reminder, we only accept cash dollars," said the boy. "An ATM machine is conveniently located in our basement." He gestured grandly toward a foreboding, half-open doorway.

"Oh God, that sketchy ATM," muttered Giovanni, when the kid was gone.

"I remember," said Cord.

"Did we have sex down there?" said Giovanni.

"I believe we did," said Cord. "Ah, the glory days."

"Yeah," said Giovanni. He took Cord's hands in his own. "But this is better."

"Is it?" said Cord. As soon as he'd strung together a year of sobriety, the pandemic had hit. Trapped at home, alone with each other, both Cord and Giovanni had agreed that a little wine would be OK. They began splitting a bottle a night, then two. Eventually, those fever-dream days of sourdough starters and banging pots outside their Upper West Side window ended, but New York—and Cord and Gio—emerged diminished, collectively sad. How had banging the pots helped the hospital workers, again? Cord's memory of those days was hazy.

Now, Cord was overwhelmed by work—as soon as 3rd Eyez had been bought for a fortune, everyone wanted Cord's firm, NYC Ventures, on their roster. But he didn't want to fund tech overlords anymore. He didn't know what he wanted to do. His latest venture, Sweethearts, was about to go public. Sweethearts used artificial intelligence to make customized chatbot spouses. ("Like the movie *Her*," the college-dropout founders had told him. "But this time, we put a ring on it!")

At Panna II, Cord's phone kept buzzing and dinging as they ordered a mixed appetizer (papadum, piazi, samosa, and banana fritter); butter chicken; lamb vindaloo; naan stuffed with cheese; naan stuffed with potato; and naan stuffed with garlic. "Should we also get the one stuffed with 'fruit and nut'?" asked Gio.

"Are you carbo-loading for a 10K?" asked Cord. "Jesus."

"We'll take that one too," said Gio.

"Wonderful, sir," said the boy, closing his waiter pad with a flourish. "I will return with your Perrier," he said.

"Thanks," said Cord. The kid removed his suit jacket, left the restaurant, ran across the street to a liquor store, and returned with a large bottle of Perrier, which he handed to a man behind the bar. The man poured sparkling water into two wineglasses and added lime wedges, and the boy put his jacket back on and delivered their drinks.

Ding! A text from Cord's business partner and college roommate, Jacobey:

SOS

Sweethearts team spinning out

Call me ASAP

"I love this restaurant," said Giovanni. "I love New York, and I love you." Gio held his glass aloft.

"Sorry, hon," said Cord. He typed: at dinner, turning off my phone.

Jacobey called. He called again. He called again.

"And we haven't set a wedding date . . ." continued Giovanni.

"We will!" said Cord. "You want to pick a date? That's fine; that's great. When?" Cord's phone buzzed again and he picked it up. "One second," he said to Gio. "Just one—Jacobey! I'll call you in an hour!"

"Get to the chopper, man," said Jacobey. "Timmy and Eddie are on MDMA and they're trying to jump off the balcony." Timmy and Eddie were the founders of Sweethearts.

"I'll be there in an hour," said Cord. "Gio's going to leave me if I don't get off the phone."

"I will," said Gio. "Honestly, I will."

"I mean, you won't," said Cord, hanging up on Jacobey.

"True," said Giovanni. "You asshole."

"I'm here, honey," said Cord. "I'm here, with you. Let's pick a date for our wedding."

Giovanni shook his head. "I have other news."

"Do tell!"

"Cord, I have planned a special vacation, and we leave on Sunday!"

"What?"

"*Return to Love,*" said Giovanni. "It's a digital detox . . . with horseback riding, canoeing, and facials."

"Sweethearts' IPO is Friday," said Cord.

"We leave on *Sunday,*" said Giovanni slowly, as if he were talking to a child.

"Did you say facials?" said Cord, touching his skin, which was in need.

"You can call Jacobey and text *whoever* and handle what you need to handle. I am going to eat my butter chicken and all the naan and then I'm going home. The resort is in the Poconos, and you're coming, and you have to put that fucking phone in a lock-box and we are going to return to love. Do you hear me, Cord Perkins? *We are going to return to love.*"

Cord's relief that he could handle his work emergency was

immense. "You won't get mad if I leave, like, now?" he said. "Even though it's our 'Day We Fell in Love'-versary?"

"I won't get mad," said Giovanni. "As long as you show up in one week for the Sunday 10:02 A.M. Greyhound from Port Authority to the 'Return to Love Digital Detox Retreat.'"

"Greyhound?" said Cord. "You mean . . . a bus?" He stood, gathering his briefcase and spring jacket, an Isaia Capri pinstripe.

"And maybe at the retreat, we can also talk about . . ." said Gio.

"I know," said Cord.

"We can detox from . . . from everything."

"I can try," vowed Cord.

19 REGAN & FRANÇOIS

Greece, three days after Savannah Country Day ended for the semester. Regan was filled with anticipation and her daughters were furious (Isabelle) and glum (Flora).

An internet boyfriend was the perfect partner for Regan during these frightening, lonely days. He texted her constantly. Regan could keep her fears from her daughters and give them all her time (as she always had). François recommended Regan take the girls to the nearby island of Hydra and the more far-flung Santorini. He helped her choose hotels and restaurants for both long weekends; when Regan pressed François to join them, he despaired that his work was crippling but would simmer down eventually. He begged Regan for photos of the sunset in Oia, grilled octopus, and Regan in a bikini.

"Oh my God, *Mom!*" Isabelle had cried, when Regan debuted the first bikini she'd worn in twenty years, emerging from the bathroom of their cliffside Santorini hotel.

"I think you look great, Mom," Flora had said. Her cheeks were pink and freckled from the sun; she'd picked up a kerchief somewhere, which she wore over two long braids. Both girls seemed lighter—and who wouldn't be? They spent their days sleeping late, scrambling over rocks down to waves, napping, eating pastries and grilled meats, and petting the stray cats that seemed to be everywhere.

"No one over forty should wear a bikini," said Isabelle. "Period, end of sentence."

"Rude!" cried Flora, stepping from their cool room, which was an actual *cave,* carved into the volcanic cliff face of Santorini's caldera. Isabelle's flip-flops slapped against stones as she ran down the winding path to the hotel's infinity pool. Flora, laughing, chased her sister. Hundreds of feet below, the sea was deep blue, dotted with tour boats that looked like toys. The girls moved through bougainvillea-draped archways, down uneven steps, past a maze of cubic white buildings with blue domes. Regan sent François a sexy selfie, scrutinizing her body in the photo, astonished at how confident she looked, how *happy.*

As always, François responded immediately, such a far cry from Matt, who had responded to her texts hours later . . . or not at all.

Stunning! wrote François. I am dreaming of standing beside you, gazing at the sea.

For the first time in her life, Regan felt like the sister who was chosen. François didn't know about Lee's magazine covers or red carpet appearances. In his eyes, *Regan* was the star. She took selfie after selfie, angling her phone to capture the light the way she'd watched Lee do countless times, finally understanding the intoxicating power of being desired.

She wrote: you have made me the person I always dreamed of being.

20 LEE

ON MONDAY MORNING, LEE'S PHONE TRILLED AT SIX A.M. SHE HAD not used her alarm in years and jerked awake, befuddled. While filming, she'd had a crew living with her and waking her with breakfast in bed. (This was part of the shtick—Lee, such a diva she needed breakfast on a tray! Though honestly, she did enjoy breakfast on a tray.) While unemployed, she'd slept past noon. And during her Savannah sojourn, Lee had roused herself around ten or eleven, padded downstairs, and poured coffee Charlotte had made into an M.A. Hadley mug, then situated herself at the counter next to her mother as they paged through *The New York Times.*

(And ignored the wall phone, ringing away.)

Lee groaned and stretched. The sun was rising outside the window of her sister's apartment, but Lee's brain felt as if she'd been hit in the head by a two-by-four.

"Auntie Lee?"

Flora approached with instant coffee. Her resemblance to her mother was so shocking that Lee felt dizzy, as if she were in one of those episodes of a TV show where a wavy screen indicates traveling back in time. She realized then, in the depths of her jet lag, that Regan had been raised to take care of her family, had gotten herself into some codependent peril, and now her own daughter was making coffee and holding it out sweetly, desperate for affection. *Family trauma,* thought Lee. *It's a bear.*

"Thanks, Flora. I can make my own coffee, though."

"Oh!" cried Flora. "I'm sorry! It's all we have, the instant. I can run to the coffee shop down the street. . . ."

"No, honey, I just meant you don't have to worry about me."

Flora blinked, perplexed. *She'd expected praise for being a martyr,* thought Lee.

"Go get ready for school," said Lee.

"I *am* ready," said Flora. She wore a pleated skirt with a blue blazer, knee-high socks, and Mary Janes. She looked like an orphan girl from a fifties movie. Lee opened her mouth to ask Flora to go wake her sister, but then realized this was how kids got "parentified." (Lee loved Instagram reels, and many of hers featured a psychologist who dressed up as a parentified child and spoke in an unsettling voice about childhood conditioning and fucked-up core memories. Lee could relate.)

She dragged herself from her sister's bed and made her way to the bathroom. She brushed her teeth, grabbed yoga pants and a top from her luggage, then slipped on shoes. Slurping the instant coffee, she rapped her knuckles on the girls' open bedroom door and called, "Wake up, buttercup!"

Isabelle opened one eye. Lee stood at the end of her bed with her arms folded over her chest. "Time to rise and shine!"

"No," groaned Isabelle, rolling away.

Lee took her long nails and dug them into the soft flesh of Isabelle's exposed shoulder.

"Ow!" Isabelle screamed, showily. "Oh my God! You scratched me!"

"It was just a poke," said Lee. "Get up. Now."

"Yikes," said Isabelle. But she got up.

It took a half hour to reach the manicured campus of the American School of Athens. "We can get out here," Isabelle growled at the gated entrance, but Lee didn't slow, waved at the guard, and entered the drop-off line. Isabelle scrunched into herself and Flora seemed pleased. When they reached the front, Lee said, "Have a good day, girls. When should I be here for pickup?"

"You don't need to—" Isabelle began.

Flora chirped, "Four!"

"Four. I'll be here."

They climbed out of the rental car that Val (blessed Val) had arranged to be delivered to Regan's apartment. "I'm going straight to the police now, girls. Please know I'm doing everything I can," said Lee. They nodded somberly, perhaps relieved to be told to focus on themselves for a change.

As Lee pulled forward, she was startled by a loud knocking on the passenger window. A teacher motioned for Lee to pull over. Had she already been recognized, even in sunglasses and a rental Hyundai? Lee moved her car out of the line.

"Sorry to bother," said the teacher, when Lee slid her window down.

"It's OK."

"Are you . . . is Isabelle . . . ?"

"She's my niece."

"Oh," said the woman, who wore the same getup as the girls, the drab, orphan-girl uniform even worse on a middle-aged woman. "I was hoping to speak to their mother."

"I'm her sister. Regan is . . . she's out of town. I'm watching the girls. How can I help?"

"Well, I just wanted you to know . . ."

The teacher was clearly nervous. Lee felt for her—it must

have been difficult to be an administrator at a school for rich kids. "Please go on," said Lee, removing her sunglasses to make eye contact.

The teacher blurted out, "Isabelle has been spending time with a young woman who doesn't go to the ASA."

"Yes?"

"This young woman lives nearby. She's been caught selling drugs to the ASA girls and sometimes . . . becomes romantically involved."

"I see."

"Yes, well, it seems that Isabelle might be this young woman's . . . newest . . . friend. And Anastasia Boosalis is problematic. She's very wealthy and . . . problematic."

"Thank you for telling me," said Lee. "I'll make sure my sister knows about this."

The woman flushed. "Anastasia is an heiress," she said. "To the Boosalis fortune? She's been expelled from several schools in the city. I believe she has a personal tutor now."

The name sounded familiar to Lee from society magazines and social media. "Thanks again," she said.

"I've heard tell of ketamine, opioids, and they crush up their Adderall pills and snort them!"

"Oh dear," murmured Lee.

"House parties in these giant mansions . . . and on their island homes!" The teacher seemed titillated . . . and maybe a bit envious. "Some of them have ski chalets in Switzerland," she continued, "and Park Avenue apartments. I'm sure there's cocaine and extremely expensive wine." The teacher stopped speaking and pursed her lips, perhaps imagining sipping a glass of cabernet in Gstaad.

"Again, thank you," said Lee, waving and rejoining the car pool lane. Truly, Isabelle's teen antics were no worse than Lee's had been. But on the other hand, Lee had grown up to be a batty actress with no family of her own . . . not even a pet! And alcohol problems ran in the family for sure. Lee thought about her brother, Cord, with a pang of sadness.

To distract herself, Lee punched "Police" into her car GPS and hit the button for "Hellenic Police Ελληνική Αστυνομία." It was seventeen minutes away, back toward downtown.

As Lee drove, her mind filled with questions: Was Regan's neighborhood called "downtown"? Would the cops speak English? Where could Regan be? What should Lee do about this drug-dealing heiress girlfriend of Isabelle's? And where could she get a strong coffee?

By the time Lee reached Hellenic Police Headquarters at 4 P. Kanellopoulou Street, the adrenaline that had powered her journey from Savannah to Athens was gone. She actually wished for a bit of anxiety, even mania, to give her the energy to push forward and find her sister.

Depression robbed Lee of agency, and her meds did the same.

She drove around and around the imposing police station, peering through her sunglasses, trying to find a parking garage. Finally, Lee spotted a likely structure, the words ΣΤΑΘΜΟΣ ΑΥΤΟΚΙΝΗΤΩΝ in neon above an entrance that led, as it turned out, into an underground space with extremely tight, spiral ramps.

Lee parked, exited on street level, and walked toward the police station, its reflective windows glinting in the bright sunlight. It was a marvel to walk down a city street unrecognized, something Lee had not been able to do anywhere in Los Angeles since the debut of *One of You to Love Me*. Every time Lee set foot in public, she was photographed . . . if not by professionals, then by the coffee barista, grocery employee, or random pedestrian she happened to interact with. It was weird being constantly documented like a rare bird. Everyone asked her for selfies, and she tried to oblige.

Lee had laughed in recognition when she read an interview with Bill Murray, during which he said, "Now what I do for a living is, I take cellphone photographs. I'm not an actor. I am a donkey that is photographed by people who don't know what to do with their cellphone camera."

Lee reached the police station, an imposing, brutalist structure. It was bright inside, with marble floors and beige walls adorned with framed photos of policemen. (Lee paused: nope, no women.) At the front desk, a young man sat in front of a digital display that cycled through public announcements, crime statistics, and news updates. The building was air-conditioned and smelled of cleaning products. "My sister is missing," Lee told the young man, and he nodded and said something in Greek. When Lee shook her head, he led her down a hallway and into a small room with two chairs and a metal table.

An older man entered the room, nodding to the first, and closing the door behind him. "Good morning, I am Astynómos— sorry, *Investigator*—Markos Papadoulos," he said. "I work with Missing Persons Division. You can call me Markos."

"Lee Perkins," said Lee.

Markos wore cotton pants and a pale blue shirt that was a bit wrinkled. His belt was brown and didn't match his black leather shoes. He used pomade in his thick hair, and his skin looked as if it would tan easily if he went in the sun, but he hadn't gone in the sun, so his complexion was ashy. He was in his late forties, maybe— around Lee's age. His nose was slightly aquiline, with a prominent bridge and downward slope that reminded Lee of the marble statues she'd seen during her trip to Rome. A bright memory flashed in Lee's mind: whirling around Rome on a golf cart tour with her family. How painfully cheesy—and incredibly fun—that had been!

"I called in a missing persons report yesterday," said Lee, forcing her mind back to the present. "For my sister, Regan Willingham. She's been living here . . . in Athens." Lee (who always watched and evaluated herself, an actor's burden) heard her own incredulity as she said "Athens." She quickly added, "I didn't mean to make that sound as if it was a bad idea for her to move to Athens, I'm sorry."

"No problem," said Markos. "Please proceed."

His English seemed good; that was a plus. "She left town last week and was supposed to return yesterday. Her phone's location app is disabled, and no one can reach her. There's no one matching her description in nearby hospitals, mental health facilities, or jails." Lee handed Markos the report Val had sent.

"I see."

"This is highly unusual." Lee spoke as if she were back on *Law & Order SVU*, where she'd had her first two speaking parts. "My sister is devoted to her girls. She'd never stay away and not be in touch."

"Do you mind if I start with the basics?"

"Of course. I mean, no. No, I don't mind." Lee arranged her facial features to read *Amiable but deeply concerned. Easy to work with and responsible . . . NOT mentally ill.*

"Please give me her full name, age, and physical description—her weight, height, hair and eye color." Lee complied, and Markos asked, "Any distinguishing features?"

"A birthmark on her right thigh," said Lee.

"And she was last seen . . . ?"

"She left home last Tuesday, saying she was going to Santorini for an artistic workshop. But my teenaged niece is a computer whiz . . . and she can't find any workshops on Santorini, or any hotel reservations in my sister's name. Her car isn't in her drive-way. In Plaka. And her phone and computer are gone."

"Do you know what your sister was wearing?"

Lee texted the girls. Isabelle sent a shrug emoji, but Flora wrote back, Mom was wearing a black T-shirt and her pink lululemon leggings. Gold sandals from Target in US. Diamond earrings, no watch.

"Do you have a recent photo? Any known threats or health issues?"

Lee texted the girls again and asked if Regan had friends to interview or if there was anyone who might have an issue with her.

She has NO FRIENDS, wrote Isabelle.

Flora sent a photo of Regan, sitting next to Flora in a nail salon. Both mother and daughter were grinning, holding up blue nail polish. Flora wrote, On my birthday! 💅

Lee scrutinized the image. "She looks thin."

"Can you tell me what her daily habits are? Any routines?"

Lee sighed. "Listen, I feel like I should bring the girls in. I just got here, to Athens."

Markos nodded. "Can you write down her social media pro-files and her phone number?"

Lee complied.

"She's a single mother?" said Markos. "Full custody?" Lee nodded. "Can you provide the ex-husband's phone number?" Lee nodded again.

"Since your sister is an adult with no health conditions, her case is classified as low risk. We'll send out an Alert Hellas, and then touch base about what's next. We can involve media—"

"No," said Lee. "Please, can we wait for any . . . media?"

Markos scrutinized her. "Why would you . . . ?" he said. He

narrowed his eyes and paused. Then he asked, "Are you a celebrity?"

"Of sorts," said Lee.

Markos nodded but didn't pry for more details, which Lee appreciated. They made arrangements for Markos to speak to the girls at a café in Plaka after school. Markos stood.

"If you think media attention would help find my sister . . ." Lee started.

Markos put his shoulders back. "Of course it would help," he said.

Lee wanted to say she would do the press conference, she did. But she just couldn't handle the flashing lights, the makeup, the transformation back into Lee Perkins, shining star. Not yet.

21 MISSING PERSON ALERT

HELLENIC POLICE HEADQUARTERS

Case #2024-MP-1047
FOR IMMEDIATE RELEASE
Contact: Lead Investigator Markos Papadoulos
Tel: +30 210 967 2437
Email: m.papadoulas@astynomia.gr

The Hellenic Police Department seeks public assistance in locating REGAN PERKINS WILLINGHAM, age 42, who was last seen April 16 at the American School of Athens (Psychiko campus) at approximately 8:15 AM.

Description:
- Height: 160 cm (5'3")
- Weight: Approximately 50 kg (110 lbs)
- Hair: Brown
- Eyes: Brown
- Distinguishing features: Freckles
- Last seen wearing: Black T-shirt, pink athletic leggings, gold sandals

Ms. Willingham's phone appears to be disabled and is missing.

Ms. Willingham is a U.S. citizen residing in Athens with her two daughters, one a minor. Family members report this disappearance is highly unusual and concerning.

Anyone with information regarding Ms. Willingham's whereabouts is urged to contact:
- Hellenic Police Department: +30 210 364 7712
- Emergency: 112
- Missing Persons Hotline: +30 210 893 7723

22 LEE

LEE AND THE GIRLS ENTERED A COFFEE SHOP CALLED CAFÉ YIASEMI, a stucco building along a street called Mnisikleous, near Regan's apartment. The door of the cozy café was surrounded by potted plants and flowers, the walls lined with wrought-iron lanterns. Above the doorway, the Greek word for jasmine—Γιασεμί—was painted in gold script.

The girls settled into the dim interior space, and—in astonishingly fluent Greek—ordered cold frappés, French fries, and slabs of some sort of tomato tart. Lee asked Flora to order her a strong black coffee, then marveled as Flora asked, "I theia mou den tis aresei o stigmiaios kafes, echete kati allo?"

Markos arrived, smelling of cigarettes, and introduced himself. As the girls answered his questions about Regan, Lee got to work on her phone trying to sort out where she could access her medications in Greece. She knew from experience that coming off bipolar meds could be a rough ride, and without her mood stabilizer, Lee would soon feel the familiar edge of hypomania creeping in. Walgreens, Lee discovered, did not exist in Greece—maybe they could transfer her prescriptions to another pharmacy.

Isabelle stood as soon as she finished her tomato tart. She said she was leaving; she had plans. "What plans?" said Lee.

"Like you care," Isabelle responded. Lee sighed, remembering her conversation with Isabelle's teacher about the bad-news heiress named Anastasia.

"I certainly do care, Isabelle," said Lee.

Isabelle acted as if she hadn't heard her aunt and exited the café, leaving her bill for Lee.

"I'm sorry my sister was rude. She's upset," said Flora. "Would you like to see the spreadsheets I made showing my mom's money transfers?"

"I certainly would," said Markos.

Lee watched Flora pull a laptop from her backpack, log into it with her face, and open an Excel document featuring highlighted columns and detailed notes. "I'm saving up to build a Framework Laptop 13," she told Markos earnestly. "I only need like fifty more euro. This school Chromebook is fine for display but I can't do anything cool on it."

Lee was proud of Flora, but the information in her spreadsheets was disquieting. Regan appeared to be sending every cent of Matt's generous child support to something called BBB Investments.

Markos said, "Can you email me these documents, please?"

"Yes, sir," said Flora.

Lee noted that Flora seemed to crave adult admiration, and felt uneasy. Flora's overzealous competence was too familiar—suddenly Lee was a teen again, sitting at the kitchen table with her father's insurance papers spread before her, creating a filing system while Charlotte stared into space and sipped her chardonnay, useless. Lee had made spreadsheets too—one for bills, one for grocery lists, one for Regan's and Cord's school schedules. Everyone had been impressed by how "together" she was, how "mature for her age."

Flora explained financial transfers to Markos with the same

forced calm Lee had once used to explain death benefits to her mother.

Depression said, *Flora is becoming you.*

Lee tried her best to ignore this horrible, if true, realization, stammering, "Well, good work, Flora! I'm sure you've given Officer Papadoulos plenty to work with."

"Have you considered a press conference, Ms. Perkins?" said Markos.

"We'll wait on that, but thank you." Lee stood to signal her farewell.

As they walked back to the apartment, Flora peered at her aunt. "You do know what those numbers mean, right, Aunt Lee?" said Flora. "Mom's been sending our child support to the scammer."

"Well, let's not jump to conclusions," said Lee, with (she heard it!) an unhinged air of gaiety.

Ugh, and Flora's face—that careful, patient expression as she waited for Lee to stop pretending! How many adults had Lee watched deny obvious truths while she stood there, sixteen and exhausted, knowing she'd have to fix everything anyway?

"Aunt Lee—"

"That's enough," said Lee. "We're going to find your mom and everything will be fine!" In her own ears, Lee sounded deranged.

Lee knew how destabilizing it was when someone pretended the truth wasn't happening. She hated bullshit, which was a rough character trait in the entertainment industry. Lee had learned to feign excitement as someone told her about a project that was almost certainly doomed; insisted they loved her show when they may have never watched it; or planned an elaborate fête that was never going to leave the group chat.

But being fake hurt, it did. Every time Lee told a falsehood or agreed to believe one, it felt like opening the wound of having had to lie for decades about her father's suicide, promising Charlotte she would say Winston had had a heart attack.

Flora looked away, obviously disappointed in her aunt. Lee couldn't blame her: She was disappointed in herself.

23 FLORA

THEIR FIRST SUMMER IN GREECE WAS VERY HOT. FLORA AND HER mother were re-binge-watching *Gilmore Girls* from beginning to end—this was how they comforted themselves in a strange city. Regan's phone made a weird, tonal sound, and Flora glanced over her mom's shoulder. She couldn't believe her eyes: Her mom was using Telegram, an app no one used for anything legal.

"Mom, is that Telegram?"

"What?" Regan flipped her phone to face the couch.

"Telegram, I saw it," said Flora.

"I've met someone, you know that," said Regan, her cheeks growing red.

"Mom! Telegram is for drug dealers."

"It's just more private than Facebook," said Regan. "You know it's not smart to put your personal information on Facebook! You—of all people—know not to trust Mark Zuckerberg!"

"What do you mean 'more private'?"

"Oh, honey. It's just a safer platform," said Regan breezily.

"It's actually not," said Flora. "What it *is* is ungovernable. If someone steals your money on Telegram, it can't be traced . . . and they can't be prosecuted."

Regan shook her head. "No one is stealing my money, honey-bee," said Regan. She put her phone in her purse and zipped it closed. "There," she said. "OK?"

Flora knew it was far from OK. There were kids at her school buying cars from scamming and making fake credit cards by punching numbers into a card with a special machine. They called their stealing "reparation," even the white ones, whose ancestors had pillaged Greece back in the day. (One of her classmates was the daughter of the museum curator who was trying to get the Elgin Marbles returned to Greece, and another classmate was the great-great-great-grandson of Lord Elgin, who had stolen them in the first place, using saws and chisels to detach and move the massive marble pieces off the Parthenon in 1800 and shipping them to England while no one was paying attention.) Flora had missed getting a perfect score on her Greek history final because she couldn't remember the name of the island where one of Elgin's marble-laden ships sank in a storm in 1804. (Flora wrote "Crete" and it was Cythera.)

Most kids at her school were rich, but some were not, and to keep up, they scammed. Punching cards was dangerous (it was a felony, after all) and complicated. Flora respected hard work. They made more money than the kids who sold pills and vape cartridges, and ten times as much as working at Starbucks or even Pizza Hut, which was a fancy restaurant in Greece (with white tablecloths!).

Flora liked to listen to Punchmade Dev and other scam rappers—she played them on her Spotify, walking around the hallways of the American School of Athens, wearing her corded headphones (earbuds were out), and learning about how scams worked. . . .

Everybody listen up, this a punch lesson.
Go and get a fire carding site, go to the dump section.

Never get a savings account dump, you always want checking.
Make sure you go and grab a credit dump, they never hit with debit.
You better put a proxy server on it or use public connection.
You can't get too comfortable on there, get the proper protection.

But Flora never thought her own mother would be scammed!

Flora called a meeting of the White Hat Hackers and biked to Starbucks Syntagma Square. They shared one Strawberry Açaí Lemonade Refresher and four cups of tap water. Flora explained that her mom was using Telegram to message her internet boyfriend.

"Romance scam," said Maya.

"Bet that," said Nico. Outside the window of Starbucks, the Hellenic Army Evzones, who guard the Tomb of the Unknown Soldier in front of the Parliament Building, started their elaborate hourly change. For a moment, the kids watched the guards in their white kilts, red tasseled hats, and red clogs. The guards lifted their legs high and kept their upper bodies perfectly still. "Has anyone ever seen an army guy smile?" said Nico.

"Not allowed," said Flora.

"Let's scambait," said Maya, tapping her index fingers together.

"What, pretend to be my mom?" said Flora.

They sat in silence for a moment. "OK," said Nico. "I mean, let's do it. Just to see if we can get any more information about him."

"Could be a woman," said Maya.

"Could be nonbinary," said Nico.

"And then we find him and contact him on our own," Maya concluded.

"We can geolocate," said Nico. "First, reverse image search."

"Yes," agreed Flora.

"Get his profile pics," said Maya.

Flora was silent. She didn't want revenge. She just wanted her mom back.

24 LEE

THE MALL ATHENS WAS A GLEAMING MONSTROSITY OF MARBLE AND glass, ten minutes from Plaka by metro. When Lee googled "pharmacy Athens English speaking," The Mall Athens website had appeared, a beacon of American-style efficiency. Surely here, in this mall that could have been in Sherman Oaks or Short Hills, she could simply refill her prescriptions as if she were at a big, air-conditioned Walgreens.

The pharmacy was on the second floor. Lee approached the counter with her empty pill bottles, arranging her face into "harried foreign woman needs help."

"Γεια σας," said the pharmacist.

"English?" Lee asked, changing her persona to "helpless but charming" in a flash.

"Of course." The pharmacist examined her bottles. "These require Greek doctor prescription."

"I completely understand. And I respect your medical system! But I do have a prescription for these medications. The number is right there on the bottle."

"Need Greek doctor, then prescriptions for you." She checked her watch. "Pharmacy closing now for lunch. Open again four P.M."

Lee felt her charm curdle. "I see," she said. "However, I really do need these medications. To be honest"—she leaned close, trying to connect, to be a "vulnerable friend" character—"I'm worried about a manic episode. I've run out of my mood stabilizer completely, and I'm almost out of my antidepressant."

The pharmacist's expression softened. "I understand, but regulations. You can wait? Talk to doctor?"

"I shouldn't wait," said Lee, truthfully. She had begun feeling mild symptoms already—she'd barely slept even though she was exhausted, and felt happier than she should, given the circumstances. Honestly, she felt better than she had in a long time, but Lee understood that feeling good was actually dangerous for her. Mania . . . such a seductive siren!

"You gonna wait," said the woman as she yanked down a metal sheet to close up shop for her four-hour (!) lunch. A piece of paper taped to the metal sheet read, NO FOREIGNERS ON TUESDAY.

Lee's off-kilter brain wondered: Is this a special message, just for me?

Lee had very thick credit cards with high limits. She exited the ol' φαρμακείο, ready for some retail therapy. The mall's architecture was aggressive in its normalcy—the same polished floors and Muzak as every mall in existence. Lee passed Zara, H&M, Marks & Spencer. Greek teenagers lounged on benches drinking Starbucks, indistinguishable from kids in Beverly Hills except for their language and the fact that they seemed to favor tighter tops.

In a department store, Lee rode the escalator up through floors of handbags and cosmetics. She sat for a makeover she didn't need, letting the artist layer thick foundation over her cheeks and chin. "You are actress?" the woman asked, and Lee neither confirmed nor denied, just smiled mysteriously, like someone in a movie.

But she was not in a movie.

Trying on a white blazer she'd never wear, Lee stared at herself under the fluorescent lights. She tossed her hair, pasted a delighted smile on her face, then realized she was alone in a dressing room, performing for absolutely no one.

She bought the blazer. And a silk scarf. And leather gloves, though it was April. With a Starbucks Lavender Latte, she sat on a bench. A small girl walked by with her mother, staring openly at Lee. Lee automatically caught the girl's gaze, and gave her a tiny, private smile: the perfect "celebrity spotted in public" expression. The girl's mother pulled her along. Lee's smile faded. She couldn't wait another two hours in this mall.

Lee gathered her bags and headed toward the metro. Tomorrow she'd try again. Or the next day. Or maybe she'd just learn to live with the price of going off her meds: no sleep, brain zaps, fabulous bursts of energy and purpose, the crushing, inevitable conclusion. At least withdrawal was real.

As she waited for the train, Lee felt ashamed of her extravagant purchases. Her sister was missing, and she'd spent the afternoon buying clothes! But at least shopping had filled the hours, made her feel like she was doing something, even if that something was just . . . making it from one second to the next.

Lee caught herself lifting her chin, resting her hand on her hip. Christ. Even alone, with no one watching, she couldn't stop being Lee Perkins, troubled actress. *But isn't she gorgeous?*

25 LEE

TWO NIGHTS LATER, LEE PASSED THE GIRLS' ROOM AND PEEKED IN. Flora was perched in front of a computer screen, her attention laser-focused, face ghostly. Lee approached, saying, "Flora, what are you up to?"

"Oh," said Flora, startled. She gestured to an onscreen video chat. "This is Maya and Nico," she said. Maya had pink hair and wore the ASA school uniform. Nico had braces and a T-shirt advertising a coding camp in Oregon. "Guys, this is my Aunt Lee," said Flora.

Lee waved at the kids, who were connected via video chat on Discord. They waved back.

"Want to see what we're working on?" said Flora.

"Of course."

Flora pointed to a photo of a handsome older man with salt-and-pepper hair and a white mustache. "This is an image of the man who Mom thinks is François," she said.

"Oh," said Lee, unnerved.

"And there actually *is* a mathematician named François Gauthier who teaches south of Paris. And this *is* his picture," said Maya.

"Wait, your mom's boyfriend is real?" said Lee, feeling relief wash over her.

Nico chimed in, "Unfortunately, no. I finally heard back from Gauthier. He has no idea who Flora's mom is. Scammers just used his photos and made a Facebook account with his name and identity, then moved Flora's mom to Telegram ASAP."

"They call people like Mom 'customers.'" Flora's voice was mechanical, treating her mom's disaster like a logic problem. Lee stared at the man on the screen.

"Jesus," said Lee, shaking her head. He was handsome, this other François. "But . . . who are *they*? And where's your mom?"

"We don't know," sighed Flora, deflated.

"*They* could be literally anyone—anywhere. Tracing cryptocurrency is possible, but these guys are pros—they're using multiple exchanges . . . I'm working on it, but I keep hitting dead ends." Maya sounded frustrated.

"Anyway, finding Mom's money might have nothing to do with finding *Mom*," said Flora, her tone still oddly detached.

"What about her phone?" queried Lee. "Did it . . . ping or whatever? Where did her fucking phone ping?"

"We're trying to get that information, but you can't just call AT&T and get it texted over," said Nico, punctiliously.

"Some *adults* should have listened the second Flora clocked her mom's disabled Find My!" said Maya.

All of the kids stared at Lee. She was the adult. But she had thought that coming to Athens was enough. Wasn't it enough? She was here! She'd involved the police! What more could she possibly do?

"Maybe a press conference could bring attention to the case," said Flora, looking steadily at her aunt.

"Goddamn it," said Lee.

26 FLORA

city streets overfull of the most random junk in the world. Everything was just piled up: Barbie dolls, hideous artwork in elaborate frames, silver, china. A retailer of mismatched chairs. A store of leather jackets and gladiator sandals. Toys, jewelry, books, lamps, musical instruments. People who had seemingly laid a sheet on the ground and piled it high with every imaginable item they could get their hands on, all of it for sale.

When they first arrived in Athens, Flora, Isabelle, and Regan had hit the flea market every weekend, buying one or two items, trying hard to "see the beauty" (as Regan put it) in tarnished lamps and scuffed furniture. Flora's mom knew how to fix a lot of things—she was crafty—and they taught themselves to sand and paint wood, found a little old Greek lady who reupholstered, and a store called Το Σπίτι του Υφάσματος ("The Fabric House"), where they browsed textiles and breathed in the smell of mothballs. Flora loved the little bell that sounded when they entered the store, loved watching her mother flip expertly through the rolls.

This was before her mother stopped leaving the apartment much at all.

Now, Flora stood in the middle of the market, feeling useless, feeling lost.

27 CORD

GIOVANNI WRENCHED CORD'S IPHONE FROM HIS HOT LITTLE HAND. "Lee and Mom have both called me," argued Cord. "Shouldn't I return their calls, and inform someone I'm going into the wilderness?"

"You can call your entire family after we return to love," said Gio, handing Cord's phone to the bald fellow at the front desk, who snapped it into a cellphone lockbox *and then* into a safe.

"Your detox begins! As soon as your Kottage is ready, I'll come find you," said the smug jerk. "Feel free to use the canoes; it's a beautiful day."

Cord followed Gio to a lakefront dock, his head aching from the whiskey nips he'd enjoyed in the Greyhound bathroom on the way to the Poconos. He and Giovanni climbed awkwardly into a wooden canoe and Gio untied them from the dock. "Phone-free in nature!" he crowed.

"I feel very ill at ease," Cord confided.

"I told Dalton I had the norovirus! This truly is a return to love."

"We met on Tinder, not in nature," noted Cord.

"Oh, pish!" said Giovanni.

"You sound like my mother," said Cord.

"Charlotte would love the Poconos," said Giovanni.

28 LEE

LEE WORE HER GUCCI SUNGLASSES TO THE PRESS CONFERENCE, hoping to shield her eyes and her psyche against the glare of the bright camera lights. Regan's heels—a size too small for Lee— were very uncomfortable. Lee angled her head downward as Markos spoke in Greek to the massive crowd of reporters and lookie-loos.

What was Markos saying? He wore a different rumpled outfit, his hair styled with even more pomade. Atop his cigarette fragrance, he'd layered a citrusy cologne (or maybe he'd eaten an orange). As he spoke, he flailed his hands around passionately. The crowd was utterly silent, hanging on his every word.

Lee watched Markos, reassured. It was nice to feel she wasn't alone in this search. As they had entered the press conference, Markos had said, "Reporters will ask about your show. About your own . . . history."

"I see," said Lee.

Markos stood at a podium adorned with the official Hellenic Police emblem—a light blue shield over a cross, with an olive branch and the scales of justice. The conference had been moved from the cramped press room to the front steps of the police station, and someone had thoughtfully set up a side table with coffee and water.

After his fevered speech, Markos gestured to her, as if she were a contestant on *The Price Is Right*. "Are you ready?" he asked, switching easily to English. "I will try to keep the questions to a minimum."

"I'm ready," Lee said. She felt the familiar shift happening—that click in her brain when Lee Perkins, the nervous mess, transformed into a star. Her spine straightened. The trembling in her hands stilled. This was what she knew how to do: Perform. Be someone else. Be someone better, no matter what it did to her to pull it off.

She stepped up to the podium. The crowd in front of her was massive, spilling across city streets and causing a traffic jam. Lee was repulsed, resigned, and also . . . thrilled.

"My sister, Regan . . ." Lee paused and took a deep breath, beginning her show. She knew exactly how to pitch her voice—not too high (hysterical), not too low (unfeeling). She'd played this role before, hadn't she? The grieving relative on *Law & Order SVU*, the worried sibling on the Lifetime movie *Slain Sister*. Lee fluttered her eyes closed, a gesture she'd perfected in her acting classes—vulnerability without ugliness—then started again, fully in "performance mode" now. This was much easier than being herself.

"My sister, Regan, is a strong mother who came to Greece to make a new life for her daughters in your beautiful, historic city." There was a murmur of appreciation. "Something has happened to my sister, and we need to get her home. Regan, if you can hear me, I want you to know that I'm going to find you. And your girls are safe with me. I'll stay until you're with them again. The girls love you. And I love you." She nodded, somber. As soon as she was silent, reporters began shouting in English and Greek:

Are there any leads?

Το τελευταίο που είδατε την αδελφή σας;

Is it true that your television show was canceled?

Is this related to your mental breakdown?

Lee froze behind the podium, alarmed. Even in her shock, Lee noticed she moved her hand toward her throat, a gesture she'd used in at least three different TV episodes to indicate *I'm distressed . . . but very sexy.*

Of course, the press knew about her hospitalization, and that she'd been hiding in her mother's gated community in Savannah to allow herself to believe she'd gotten through her recovery unrecognized.

The careful character she'd constructed cracked—underneath was just Lee: mentally ill, washed-up, desperate for attention.

Markos stepped in front of the microphone, holding up a palm in a gesture to stop the barrage of questions. "Regan Willingham's disappearance is unrelated to her sister's job. Lee Perkins is here in Athens to assist the search. No questions at this time," he said. Lee moved back to the microphone. "You do not have to say anything," said Markos, furrowing his brow as if he wanted to add, *Please don't.*

But Lee needed one more second in the spotlight. "Please help me find my little sister!" she said. She burst into tears, allowing the cameras to flash. "Help us, please," she breathed, a perfect last whisper.

Markos put an arm across her shoulders and steered her away from the podium. Lee wanted to fight him and stay in front of the crowd, but his grip was tight. She inhaled, showily, even *that* calculated for the cameras, and turned away from her rapt audience.

The press conference, and Lee's calculated breakdown, would reach everywhere, including Hollywood.

29 LEE

AFTER SHE WALKED OUT OF THE PRESS CONFERENCE, LEE ASKED Markos where she could "powder her nose," an insipid euphemism that Charlotte had taught her daughters to use, because *God forbid* a woman mention her bodily functions or wish for privacy. Lee needed to be alone . . . just for a minute, offstage.

Markos pointed her down a side hallway with a polite nod. The door to the women's WC was unmarked aside from a fading stick figure in a skirt. *How apt,* thought Lee, pushing open the door to a utilitarian room tiled in white squares.

The sink had two taps: "Z" and "K." Lee vaguely remembered from her sister's bathroom that "K" was "kryo," cold. (She later discovered that "Z" was "zesto," for a zesty, hot shower.) It felt good to run water over her hands. The window above the stalls was open a crack, letting in the ambient chorus of Athens: horns, mopeds, passionate shouting in a language she could not decipher.

There she was, cloudy in an old mirror above the sink: Lee Perkins, superstar.

She'd done it again—made her eyes vulnerable, let her voice break at the perfect moment as she said, *Help us, please.* Even in genuine terror about her sister, she'd automatically performed grief like the trained seals she'd once seen on a school trip to SeaWorld Orlando.

And the most damning thing was that for those few minutes in front of the cameras, with everyone hanging on her words, she'd felt supremely alive, even verging on *happy*. Lee gripped the edge of the porcelain sink. She'd sworn she was here to find Regan, but she'd just used her sister's disappearance to score a hit of attention. The pattern was gross and obvious: Create a crisis or find one, swoop in as savior, thrive on feeling essential. Then what?

Then nothing.

Then back to the gnawing emptiness.

She was still that fifteen-year-old girl who'd just found her father's body, the one who tried to convince herself that tragedy made her special. (As opposed to just . . . tragic.) A weight settled on Lee's chest. The high of being needed was already fading, leaving her emptier than ever.

30 LEE

3

MARKOS GUIDED LEE UNNOTICED THROUGH A BASEMENT DOOR TO the parking garage, then drove her back to Regan's apartment. "We're getting many calls now," said Markos. "I can only hope one is a credible lead. It was brave of you to speak."

"Thank you," Lee managed. Her mind was racing, her skin electric . . . as if tiny shocks were running just beneath the surface. When she turned her head too quickly, light outside the car window lagged behind her vision and made her dizzy. Her brain chemistry was definitely off.

It had taken months to get the right balance. A doctor had shown her a chart, the way her moods could veer frighteningly high, then dangerously low. She had to be watchful, the doctor insisted. "If you don't take these medications religiously," he said, "you need to understand that mania will return . . . and eventually, so will suicidal ideation. I want you to buy one of those plastic pillboxes, with the days and 'AM' and 'PM.' Do you promise me, Lee? This matters. I want you to live a full life, and you can, but if you mess with the meds, your moods will get out of control fast."

"I promise," Lee had said, picking at the wrist of her mental hospital sweatsuit. She had meant it, had been very careful since her release. But how could she anticipate an entire country with no Walgreens? "Markos," said Lee. "Can I ask you something?"

"Hm?"

"I need to talk to a Greek doctor. Could you help me . . ." She intended to ask him if he could help her find a psychiatrist, but he was staring straight ahead as if he hadn't heard her. "Markos?"

"I'm sorry, I am distracted," he said. "My apologies. What were you saying?"

"Oh," said Lee. "Nothing, never mind." She fell silent as he drove toward Plaka. The last few blocks were narrow and cobbled. "You can drop me here," said Lee.

"No, it's OK," said Markos. He ignored the PEDESTRIAN ONLY signs, drove straight to Regan's door. "I'll be in touch," he said, putting the car in Park.

"I'm not brave, actually," said Lee.

"I disagree," said Markos.

"I don't have a choice," said Lee. "People want to watch dramatic things. If I can bring attention to Regan, if I can find her, I'll do anything."

Markos nodded. "I would do the same," he said.

As he spoke, Markos seemed preoccupied, gazing fixedly at a spot over her shoulder. *Typical chauvinist,* thought Lee. "Good night," she said.

"My apologies," said Markos, looking straight at her. "I'm nervous to be around you because my job is to treat you like a normal person and you are . . . extraordinary."

To be honest, Lee heard this a lot. But it was nice, coming from this man in his rumpled clothes. Weird, badly timed . . . but nice. "Thank you for helping find Regan," she said softly, being kind but also distant. She had one goal in Greece and it was to make sure her sister was safe. "Please let me know as soon as you have any news. Anything," she said. Markos nodded.

Lee stepped from the car and walked to Regan's locked door, pressed the bell. Flora let her inside and Lee practically collapsed once she was in the apartment. "I need to sleep," she moaned.

"Why did you cry and stuff on TV?" said Flora.

"I thought it would make people talk," said Lee.

"Smart," said Flora. "Do you want some tea, Auntie Lee?"

"You know, calling me 'Auntie' makes me feel old," said Lee.

"I mean, you kind of are old," said Flora, turning on the kettle.

Lee laughed. While Flora made tea, Lee looked through her phone at the coverage of the press conference. In every image, she was positioned for the camera, her despair artful. "I always know where the cameras are," Lee mused.

"What?"

"I did the press conference to help find your mom. But look at me. Look at my face." Lee enlarged her own anguished visage on her phone screen.

Flora came to her aunt's side and studied the photo. "You look sad."

"I look like an actress *playing* sad."

Flora was quiet for a moment. "Mom does that too. Performs, I mean. Even when she's alone."

"Yeah?"

"She takes selfies constantly. Like she's trying to prove she exists."

"Ugh, that sounds about right," said Lee. "I wish I knew how to just . . . be here."

Flora was silent, then said, "I wish someone would see me."

Flora's words were sudden, and out of left field. It took Lee a moment to process them. She turned to look, really look, at her niece. Flora's hair was thin and stringy. She needed to see a dermatologist: Her skin was a mess of pimples across her nose and along her chin. Depression, quiet for days, stirred: *You can't save her. You can't even save yourself.*

"I . . . like your shirt," said Lee lamely.

Flora looked down at her faded pink top. "Thanks," she said. Lee could almost hear the words left unspoken: *Thanks for nothing.*

31 CORD

"WAIT—I THOUGHT WE JUST NEEDED TO PUT THE PHONE IN THE lockbox *during the day!*" protested Cord, using his plastic wristband to open the door to Kiss Me Kottage #12. Inside, a fire was blazing and a buffet of aphrodisiacs had been set out: oysters, avocados, figs, watermelon, and honey. A warm teapot had a printed sign inviting them to sip "Maca Root Tea, a known adaptogen that enhances stamina and libido." On the bed, Cord saw a cat toy with a feather and silk handcuffs.

"I did the tantric workshop," argued Cord. "I did the 'Swipe Right into My Arms' ballroom dancing class! I thought I'd at least get my phone after dinner."

"Ballroom dancing *was* awkward," admitted Giovanni. "And the nutrient-dense loaf at dinner . . ." He winced, then went to the bed and picked up the cat toy. "Meow," purred Gio. "Come here, kitten."

"Look, Gio. I just need my phone for a few minutes. What if something's happened to my mom? Or your mom? I just want to scroll the news . . . just for twenty minutes? I should check in with the Sweethearts team about the IPO. . . ."

"You are not," pronounced Giovanni, using the feather toy to punctuate his statement, "as important as you think you are, Cord!"

"That's not very nice," Cord responded, stung. "I'm just going to go check in with humanity and then I'll lock up the phone again and come back."

"Cord! This— *This* is humanity!" Gio gestured to the bed, the tea, and the sexy snacks with the feathered cat toy. "Here I am!"

"I'm sorry, sweetheart." Cord lifted his hands, penitent but resolute. "I have a job, Gio. We have elderly mothers!"

Giovanni scoffed. "The theater kids at Dalton think I have the norovirus," he said. "And I told my family I was going on a wellness retreat and I'd call in ten days. You can do this, Cord."

"Oh, I see. I should tell the Sweethearts team I won't check in about the IPO because I'm sick?"

"Whatever you have to do," said Giovanni.

"I've been literally shaking all day," Cord disclosed.

Giovanni nodded. "Detoxing," he said, in a know-it-all tone that made Cord want to slug him.

"I drank all my hidden nips already."

"Let's go get a DVD and some popcorn from the Fun Library," said Giovanni, perusing the *Return to Love* daily planner. "Or we can stargaze with Sheila, arrange flowers with Pam, or have sex!"

"I used to read books," mused Cord, staring out the Kottage window at the impossibly black sky. "I'd open a book and just . . . read it."

"Imagine," said Giovanni dryly, crossing his arms over his chest.

But all Cord could imagine was the dozens—hundreds—of electronic notifications surely shining on his phone, ready to prime his dopamine transmitters to pump out some of that serenity, that buzzy calm. He yearned to check his phone. He desired his phone more than his Giovanni, and that was, he knew, a problem. The only other way he knew to soothe himself was booze.

"Go for a long, hard run," his AA friends would say. "Do an insane kettlebell class!" Neither worked for Cord.

He knew Giovanni was trying to salvage their relationship. And he did not want to be alone. He loved Giovanni, truly and forever. He was just a damn mess. But he had to try—*he had to try.* "Can we snuggle?" asked Cord.

"Come here," said Giovanni. He lifted their coverlet and patted the soft sheets, smiling. Cord crawled into the cozy spot next to the love of his life. He tried to rest.

32

LOS ANGELES TIMES
Entertainment & Arts

REALITY STAR LEE PERKINS EMERGES
IN GREEK MYSTERY
Appears disheveled and emotional at
press conference in Athens, Greece
By Helena Chen
Entertainment Reporter

Lee Perkins, whose raw struggle with manic depression made *One of You to Love Me* must-watch reality TV, has surfaced in Athens, Greece, searching for her missing sister, and sources say the story behind the disappearance is raising eyebrows.

Perkins, 43, whose public breakdown during her show's final season drew record ratings, appeared disheveled at a police press conference yesterday in central Athens. Her sister, Regan Willingham, is reportedly missing in Greece.

"Lee is completely focused on her family during

this crisis," says her agent, Francine Bloom. "Although she's being courted for several prestigious projects, her only concern is finding her sister."

Adding another layer of Hollywood intrigue, Perkins's ex-boyfriend Jason O'Brien has just been cast as Lord Byron in Ben Morris's biopic, *Mad, Bad, and Dangerous to Know*. O'Brien, who dated Perkins before her reality show debut, was contacted at his Hollywood Hills home but declined to comment.

"The whole thing is pretty wild," says an industry insider. "Lee was famous for baring her soul on TV, and now her sister's missing in a foreign country. It's like reality TV came to life."

Greek authorities declined to comment on an ongoing investigation.

33 FLORA

ON WEEKDAYS, FLORA WOKE AT 6:47 A.M., ALLOWING HERSELF EX-actly thirteen minutes to shower and get dressed before she needed to leave for school. She slipped out of bed and padded to the bathroom, stepping carefully over the floorboard that creaked. Everyone had always told her not to bother Auntie Lee, who was unstable, so until her mom came home, Flora had decided to take care of herself.

She showered quickly, braided her hair while it was still damp, and put on her school uniform. She'd adjusted to her silent morning routine—no hair dryer, no cabinet doors slamming. In the kitchen, she made herself toast with honey and poured orange juice into a travel mug. She packed her lunch: a sandwich with the good cheese, an apple, some crackers. She left a note on the counter.

Gone to school, love, Flora

The walk to the metro station was her favorite part of the day. Athens was waking up around her, shopkeepers rolling up their metal shutters, old men settling in at café tables with tiny cups of coffee and thick newspapers. Sometimes Flora pretended she was a character in a movie, a mysteriously independent teenager who navigated foreign cities with effortless grace. In the movie version, someone would notice how mature she was.

Someone would think she was remarkable.

34 LEE

LEE CHECKED IN EVERY DAY WITH MARKOS. HE TOLD HER HE WOULD call if there was news . . . and he didn't call. She contacted three psychiatrists: Two didn't speak English and the English-speaking one couldn't see her for two and a half months.

Lee caught herself checking her appearance in every reflective surface—the coffeepot, the window, the TV screen when it was turned off. Even when she was by herself in the apartment, she ruthlessly scrutinized her forehead for wrinkles, narrating a running critique of her looks and performance.

On Sunday morning, Lee's phone finally chimed with a text from Markos. We need to speak in person as soon as possible. Lee arranged to meet him at the taverna on the corner, donning a black top (to convey *somber*) and expensive jeans (*rich, fit, too concerned about my sister to worry about clothes*).

Markos was smoking outside the café. As Lee approached, he dropped his cigarette to the cobblestoned street and ground it out with a leather ankle boot. "Sorry," he said, "I can't seem to quit." He wore a tailored gabardine trench coat over a light blue button-down shirt (a bit frayed at the collar), a messenger bag, and dark jeans.

"There are worse habits," said Lee.

"I have them all," said Markos, looking rueful. He had circles under his deeply set eyes. Even when clean-shaven (Lee could smell an astringent aftershave), his cheeks were shadowed with stubble.

"I doubt that," said Lee. "OK, what's the news?" Noticing that her hands were trembling slightly, Lee clasped them together. The headache that had started three days ago pulsed behind her temples. She'd woken twice last night drenched in sweat, her heart racing: withdrawal. Markos tipped his head to the side and furrowed his brow, looking at her. "You are OK?" he said— a statement that functioned as a question.

Lee was unaccustomed to anyone wondering how she was feeling. She was trained to project emotions, not wallow in them. In truth, Lee was not OK. She was overwhelmed and teary. She wanted to cry, yearned for the release of just sobbing on this man's shoulder. She wanted him to hold her, to hold her up. She figured these desires were caused by chemical imbalances in her brain. She didn't even know this gruff Greek detective.

Lee had never gone for classic male beauty—she chose lovers who were broken in body and spirit, men (and a few women) whom she could allow to treat her badly because she pitied them and wanted to save them. But Markos seemed strong—he was a man to lean against, not to save.

Lee knew how to make herself cry for a camera—she just thought about her father as a boy, alone and disconsolate. She thought about her mom, Charlotte, a hopeful girl before she was taken advantage of in her young teens by a famous painter. (At least according to an essay Charlotte had written to win them the Mediterranean cruise on the *Splendido Marveloso* ship.)

When trying to summon tears for the camera, Lee was not

able—not yet—to access how she, herself, had felt as a child, but she had been trained to channel others' sorrow (which felt nothing like Depression).

Lee cleared her throat, shook herself to attention. "What is it, Markos?" she said. "You told me you needed to meet."

"Let's walk," said Markos. He put his hands in his pockets and began striding down the narrow street lined with small shops and tavernas. Lee was glad she'd pulled on Regan's sneakers—Markos walked quickly. The road became more residential as it wound between buildings painted in cream and ocher, many covered with ivy vines and some boasting balconies lined in pots of blooming flowers. "We've found your sister's car at Athens International Airport."

Lee stopped walking. "She flew somewhere? Where? When?"

"We're fast-tracking a warrant to access passenger information."

"But that could take—"

"Days, yes. Possible, a week or more. I'm sorry."

"Oh my God."

"We've completed interviews with all of her former Airbnb tenants. Every one has a credible alibi; we don't think they are involved."

Lee nodded. With Flora's help, she had shut down the Airbnb rental page for the time being.

She was growing short of breath, but kept pace with Markos, hiking a steep path lined with white houses. The exertion made her notice that her legs were shaking, too. Everything felt unstable—not just her emotions, but her actual body. She stumbled slightly, and Markos steadied her. "Where are we?" said Lee, slowing down, smelling jasmine, bougainvillea, and the earthy scent of the sun warming the stones beneath them. Each home had vivid, bright blue doors and window shutters.

"This is Anafiotika," said Markos.

"I don't even feel like I'm still in Athens," said Lee. "This looks like a magazine spread of a Greek island up here. My family went to Rhodes Island, on a cruise."

"A cruise?" said Markos, raising his eyebrows.

"My mom won a contest, and the prize was a Mediterranean cruise," said Lee. "It's a long story, for another time."

Markos nodded. Lee wanted to take his hand. Was this some kind of trauma response?

"The workers who built this neighborhood were from the island of Anafi," said Markos, speaking while he allowed Lee to catch her breath. "They built their homes as their ancestors had done."

Lee looked around at the whitewashed homes.

"My grandmother was from Anafi," said Markos. "This is my neighborhood."

High above the city, Lee could hear birds and the rustling of leaves. Markos pointed to a vacant building. "This building was once our family bakery," said Markos. "My parents were tricked, while I was in college."

"Tricked?"

"An investment that did not exist. They lost everything believing in a lie."

"Like Regan."

"Yes. This matters to me."

Lee gazed at the sweeping views from Anafiotika, the sun warm on her face. The Acropolis towered above them, and the city was spread out below.

"Why are you telling me this?" Lee asked.

"Because I want you to understand—I'm not trying to use your fame to solve this case." Markos met her eyes. "I see someone in pain trying to help her sister. That's all." Lee was disarmed—

Markos genuinely seemed to care. When was the last time someone had been nice to her without wanting something?

Markos was so straightforward and earnest . . . it made Lee suspicious. Was his candor a cultural thing?

Lee was accustomed to being prized for her external beauty and connections. But being treated with dignity confused her. Lee was filled with conflicting desires: She wanted to press Markos against the wall of his family's former bakery and kiss him. Also, she wanted to run.

Instead, she spoke as earnestly as Markos had. "I found my father," Lee said, the words emerging before she could stop them.

Markos held her gaze.

"When I was fifteen. He had killed himself in my bathroom. Hung himself." Lee kept her voice steady, reciting facts. "I found him before school. I called 911, then went downstairs and made breakfast for my sister and brother. Mom told them he'd had a heart attack. Only my mom and I knew what he had done."

She waited for the usual response—the awkward sympathy, the change of subject. But Markos asked, "What did you make them for breakfast?"

His unexpected question caught Lee off guard. "What?"

"For breakfast. What did you make?"

"Cinnamon toast," Lee said, remembering. "It was the only thing I knew how to cook besides scrambled eggs, and we were out of eggs."

Markos nodded thoughtfully. "My father walked out on my mother when I was twelve. I also made breakfast for my sisters and brothers. Bread with olive oil."

"I've never told anyone about making breakfast," Lee said. "It seemed . . . I don't know. Trivial—compared to finding my dad."

"Not trivial," said Markos. "It's the moment you became

someone who takes care of others. You've been doing it ever since, yes?"

Lee was moved by his insight. She had spent her life alternating between control and chaos, always trying to manage others' emotions while her own threatened to drown her.

"My old therapist would charge three hundred dollars for that observation," she said. Her mind returned to Regan. "I keep thinking about what I could have done differently. If I'd visited my sister, called her more . . . how could I not have known what she was getting into?"

"She's an adult," said Markos. "Why would you feel responsible?"

"It's just who I am," said Lee.

Markos leaned forward. "Lee, you are here now, fighting for her."

Her dark thoughts taunted her: *He's just saying what you want to hear.*

But when she looked at Markos, Lee saw no deception or agenda. Markos seemed to understand loss and responsibility.

"I'm scared all the time," said Lee softly. "Not just about Regan. About . . . everything. My brain tells me terrible things."

"Like what?" Markos asked.

Lee hesitated. "Like . . . my family would be better off without me. Like, I'll never feel peace. Finding Regan won't even change anything because I'll still be . . . I'll still feel this way."

She waited for him to offer platitudes. Markos kept his eyes on her face. "This voice," he said finally. "Is it telling you the truth?"

"It feels like the truth."

"Possible, this voice is a liar," said Markos.

Lee felt a small space opening between herself and Depression's relentless narrative. She nodded. "Possible," she acquiesced.

"As soon as the warrant comes through," said Markos, "we'll know which flight Regan was on and where she went."

Lee nodded.

"I cannot promise what condition she will be in, Lee," said Markos. "But I promise we will not stop looking." Lee stared at Markos, hearing Depression's warning: *Don't trust him. Don't be vulnerable.*

She thought of a quiet rebuttal: *Possible, this voice is a liar.*

Her chest grew warm, and her stomach eased. For a moment, hope flickered inside Lee. Markos's hand found hers (finally), and he held her fingers.

Possible, she would feel peace.

Lee caught sight of their reflection in the front window of a cottage: grieving woman being comforted by handsome cop. Even now, she was arranging herself for an imagined audience. Embarrassed, Lee pulled her hand away.

35 LEE

DAYS PASSED—WHY WAS THE WARRANT TAKING SUCH A LONG TIME to reveal any information from the flight manifests? When Lee complained, Markos told her Greece was a slow-moving bureaucracy. Lee suspected, too, that a missing, middle-aged American just wasn't a priority. Crime shows implied that police departments dropped everything to focus on a single case, but Markos was not Mariana van Zeller; Regan's disappearance not a *Trafficked* episode.

Lee discovered a dull and exhausting sense of purpose trying to take care of the girls, her admiration for Regan growing by the hour. How had Regan tackled the sink full of dirty dishes day after day? The trash bag full to bursting, teenaged dirty clothes everywhere, counters somehow splattered with tomato sauce *and* spilled milk? No wonder Lee's sister had craved an internet thrill!

After dragging the garbage to the street one night, Lee sat on the couch next to Flora, who was clicking through her mother's camera roll on her own computer. (Flora and her crew had accessed the images as soon as Regan didn't return home; they'd been por-ing over them since, to no avail.) Lee winced, gazing at Regan's badly lit selfies. Regan had lost weight; she looked wan and des-perate. In many of the photos, she was holding her hair back to show a pair of diamond earrings.

"What's the deal with the earrings?" muttered Lee, thinking of the empty jewelry box in Regan's bedside table drawer.

"She got all these stupid gifts from him." Flora's shoulders fell forward a bit. "I talk about François like he's a *person,*" she said, disgustedly.

Lee had often wondered if *she* were really a person—or just the character named Lee Perkins that she played on her "reality" show. For example: Right now, Lee felt as if she were in some sort of crime drama, playing a concerned aunt helping a worried child find her mother. Yet putting her arm around Flora had been in-stinctual; Flora's head on Lee's shoulder was true.

But it also would have looked good for the television crew.

"I should have asked more questions when she said she'd met someone," sighed Lee.

"It's not like you guys are close," said Flora.

"Ouch," said Lee.

"But it's true, Auntie Lee, right?"

Lee shrugged. "I guess," she said. "Yeah."

Flora looked vulnerable, despite her brash tone. Lee knew the feeling of wishing fervently for an adult, then realizing you were the only adult in the room. What would teenaged Lee have wanted, during all the years she only had selfish Charlotte for a parent?

"You're not alone in all this," said Lee.

Flora's eyes were wary.

"Come on, let's tuck you in."

"I'm sixteen, Aunt Lee," scoffed Flora. Still, she followed when

Lee headed to the room Flora shared with her older sister, who was not in her bed.

"Where's Isabelle?" said Lee.

"Probably with Anastasia," said Flora. "Or her boyfriend. She's pansexual."

This was more than Lee felt capable of parsing at the moment. She folded back Flora's covers and Flora climbed in. Lee tucked the blankets around Flora as she had once done with Regan and Cord. "Little burrito," she said.

Flora closed her eyes and smiled.

Lee went into Regan's kitchen, where the Acropolis was visible from a window above the sink: golden-hued columns above a rocky plateau, surrounded by ancient fortifications. She had never felt so far away from Savannah, which was (Lee knew) what Regan had been going for.

How had Regan's new life gone terribly wrong?

"Are you alive, Reeg?" Lee whispered.

There was no answer.

Lee made a cup of tea and went out on the balcony. The Athenian dusk was beginning—that magical hour when the city transformed from blazing white to rose gold. The marble columns of the Parthenon caught the last rays of sun, glowing like lit candles against the deepening sky. Church bells rang across the neighborhood, mixing with the call of swifts diving between buildings. Even the air was changing, the day's heat lifting to reveal the cool breath of the sea.

Lee sat in one of three primary-colored chairs and heard a loud bark. Across the street, she saw a medium-sized dog, a Samoyed . . . or maybe a husky. The dog's abundant coat—once pure white, she imagined—was grayish near the paws, yellowed along its back. The corners of its mouth were slightly upturned and its triangular ears perked up. The dog was staring intently at Lee, as if it were trying to convey a warning. Beneath its fur, the dog was way too thin. The animal's fixed scrutiny cast a spell on her—there was a message she wasn't understanding.

Yet.

36 LEE

THE DOORBELL RANG AGAIN AND AGAIN. LEE GROANED, CHECKED her phone—it was 3:04 A.M.—and climbed from bed. "It's me, Auntie Lee!" yelled Isabelle through the intercom. Lee buzzed her in and unfastened the three apartment locks. Isabelle lurched in the door, reeking of booze and cigarettes, clutching her girlfriend's hand. "Anastasia and I are in love," Isabelle slurred. "We are in love and we don't care who knows it!"

"That's wonderful. Can you keep your voice down?"

"We are in love," Anastasia repeated, pronouncing each syllable carefully. Anastasia had a Britishy, overenunciated accent and jet-black hair that fell in a glossy sheet to her mid-back. She was skinny with a pudgy nose, her eyebrows plucked to thin, arched lines. Her blood-colored lip stain had gotten on her teeth (unless her teeth were bleeding?) and she kept tugging at her tight velvet tube dress. "We are in love," she repeated, speaking each syllable with care.

Lee had been warned that Anastasia was a threat, but she seemed like yet another lost kid. The girls stood defiantly, as if someone were about to argue against their union, but Lee shrugged, too tired to point out their obvious intoxication. "We are not drunk," said Anastasia, as if reading Lee's mind.

"I haven't had an-ny-thing al-co-hol-ic," said Isabelle with concentration, beaming when she got the sentence out clean.

Lee sighed. The girls reminded her of how wild she had been—her chaos had once intrigued those around her, especially her ex-boyfriend Jason. They had met at a riverside bonfire. Someone dared Lee to throw her shirt into the fire. Later, she chipped her tooth swigging whiskey. Jason had looked at her, topless with an imperfect smile, and said, "You're the only real thing at this party."

Lee sighed, missing the days when her crazy behavior seemed fun. She studied Isabelle—grinning, glassy-eyed, tucked under Anastasia's arm—and felt . . . jealous. In her youth, Lee had also been loud, adored, and brave.

The world had made her pay for it.

"I think it's time for Isabelle to go to bed," Lee said, forcing calm into her voice, "and for you, Anastasia, to head home. I can call you an Uber."

"No," said Anastasia defiantly. "I'm not leaving Isabelle."

Isabelle leaned her head on Anastasia's shoulder, eyes closing. "Come on, baby," Anastasia whispered, guiding Isabelle down the hall. "Thanks, Mrs. Perkins," she called over her shoulder.

Lee followed them slowly, then kept walking to her sister's room. As she tried to fall back asleep, she remembered the girl she used to be.

37 REGAN & FRANÇOIS

FRANÇOIS WANTED REGAN TO BE ONLINE AND IN CONTACT WITH HIM at all times. He followed her on her phone's Find My app, which at times felt protective to her, and at times felt as if she were being monitored like an errant child. But every time she felt uncomfortable, she tamped it down. Without François, she had nothing but empty days. She would be forced to reckon with shame—had coming to Athens just been one big mistake? No, no, Regan had to move forward. She had to believe in this new life, in her own sense of possibility, and in François. One morning, she went for a jog around Plaka, making sure her ringtone and tracking app were on.

She huffed and puffed and her old sneakers pinched, and she was thirsty. After what felt like ten million years, she stopped in the middle of a busy street and bent forward, gasping, her hands on her hips and her head down. There was a nice breeze on the back of her neck. "Lady, you OK?" asked a vendor selling gold leaf headbands (his sign read, BE LIKE ATHENA) and evil-eye jewelry.

"Yes," said Regan. She stood, tightened her ponytail, and looked at her watch. She had been jogging for twenty minutes. Regan entered a shop, letting the air-conditioning wash over her. She leaned into a rack of Acropolis merch and knocked it over. Fifteen-euro T-shirts on hangers clattered to the floor.

"I'm sorry," said Regan, staring at the mess.

"Is OK, is OK," said an older woman with hair dyed pumpkin orange. She glared at Regan and shook her head, then lit a cigarette.

Regan started crying.

"I said, is OK," said the woman, irritated.

Regan muttered—again!—that she was sorry, hurrying out of the store. She ran all the way home, and it took her twelve minutes. Why was she crying?

Inside her bedroom, which smelled strongly of the rosemary potpourri Flora had placed on her mother's bedside table, Regan tried to sift through her feelings. She was jogging to lose the weight she'd gained since moving to Greece. She wanted to look even better than her decade-old photo on Facebook. François had said he was talking to a therapist about his fear of Regan seeing him on a video call.

Regan opened Telegram. She scrolled through François's morning greetings, his compliments, his questions about her day, his growing alarm that she had not responded for twenty minutes.

I was jogging! she wrote.

Good for you! I have big news, wrote François.

Regan waited, watching the secret chat window. She was still teary from her awkward encounter with the orange-haired woman, but had stopped actively sobbing. It was hard to admit how much she yearned for some big news. Big news! None of the private school moms ever had big news. The news, when she'd attended the PTA Coffee, was about home renovations, school events, and skin care. And—always—the husbands. None of the ASA moms liked their husbands much. Regan had known these women for months and had never heard a big surprise from any of them.

What is it? Regan typed.

She waited. François did not respond. She stood up and decided she would take a shower. She would be offline for maybe six minutes: That would show him!

When Regan stepped out of the shower onto her lush mono-grammed bath mat (she'd mailed her bath linens from Savan-nah), her phone was bright with messages. Regan dried her hand and grabbed the device.

I'm coming to visit!

Hello?

I booked a ticket.

Are you there?

Regan?

Hello?

My love?

You don't want me to come.

Regan hurried to text him back, terrified of losing her connec-tion to hope. She felt the stomach pain she had felt when she had left Mr. Ragdale behind in the motel room in the bad place where he had taken her. She had escaped but the pain, the end of hope, it was unbearable—she typed as fast as she could:

I'm here!

Sorry was in the shower!

> Best news ever! I can't
> believe it!

He wrote:

> You did not respond.

> I decided you did not want me to
> come.

> I canceled my ticket.

Regan inhaled, her stomach seizing as if she'd been sucker punched. She texted François back furiously, repeatedly, her body flooding with adrenaline. But he did not answer. Regan paced her apartment. She couldn't eat. He was actually going to come see her and she had ruined everything. She was such an idiot. Such an idiot. She hated herself.

How many times could she apologize?

Many, many times.

But for now, François—and his attention, his love—was gone.

38 CHARLOTTE

CHARLOTTE PERKINS DIDN'T HAVE MUCH TO DO IN SAVANNAH BE-
sides drive her golf cart around Palmetto Shores fretting about
her daughter. On Sunday, Charlotte decided to go to mass. Easter
was still a while away, but as she dressed in an ivory pantsuit,
Charlotte considered what she was going to give up for Lent.
Maybe pickles! She'd never given up pickles before, and while she
did like a tangy spear next to a grilled hot dog at the pool, she
could make do for the Lord Jesus Christ.

(She could get onion rings.)

Charlotte had been brought up by very strict and worried
Catholics and, after one summer of erotic adventures in France,
had become a strict and worried Catholic herself. As a child growing up in exclusive boarding schools where she'd been given very
little love or empathy, she'd been overwhelmed by constant guilt,
guilt that persisted to this day.

What the heck did Charlotte Perkins have to be guilty about?
Nothing, that's what! She was just an old lady eating Triscuits and
cheese, watching the Turner Classic Movies channel. And yet, the
sense that she was bad and in the wrong rarely left her. She went
to confession at St. James the Less, droning on about her petty
indiscretions, her naughty thoughts, and how she sometimes

wished her children were different—and frankly, better—people. Much of the time, she could bear the guilt. It rubbed against her heart like a pebble and she was used to it.

But Easter, Lord above! For Catholics (at least Catholics in Charlotte's family network) Easter was the High Holiday of Guilt. I mean, Jesus had allowed himself to be nailed to a cross for Charlotte Perkins's sins. Her mother, Louisa, cold and snooty on the best of days, had taken her harsh parenting to a new level over the Easter holidays.

While smoking Parliaments, her posture erect, Louisa would opine: Egg hunts were gauche, jelly beans emblematic of America's sugar addiction, and "don't even get me started on those revolting marshmallow Peeps!"

Charlotte, who returned "home" infrequently, was slavishly devoted to her distant mother throughout her early years, starved for any scrap of maternal affection. Thus, she agreed with her mother enthusiastically when Louisa venomously attacked anything she deemed "childish," "frivolous," or "American."

Charlotte was, of course, an American child who yearned for *fun:* As Louisa spoke and her daughter nodded vehemently, Charlotte began to dig herself into the hole of self-hatred where she'd remained ever since.

Charlotte's own three children were rarely allowed Easter treats, hunts, parties with grown men dressed as pink bunnies, or those weird egg-dye kits with the wire holder that you dipped into colorful vinegar. What did any of these American activities have to do with Jesus? The Perkins kids chose what they would forgo for Lent (Lee skipped sugar, Cord denied himself Coke, and Regan tried—and failed—to give up her greatest pleasure: warm glazed donuts) and went to mass.

She taught them ruthless self-examination. The confessional, an ornate wooden cabinet, smelled of polish and sweat. Father

Ambrose breathed audibly through the honeycombed screen. The children confessed, and received penance.

"I'm eight," Cord said once. "I don't have any sins."

"Then you're not being honest with yourself," Charlotte told him. *"Everyone* has sinful thoughts."

"Maybe thinking I don't have any sins *is* my sin," said Cord, seriously.

"Good boy," Charlotte assented.

She'd indoctrinated her children out of fear. Truly, Charlotte believed that sinners would go to hell. Even the sermons of Father Thomas—before he had moved dioceses, breaking Charlotte's heart—featured the hell that awaited them if they turned away from God. "Do you want to be exiled for eternity from the source of all goodness, love, and joy?" Father Thomas would ask from the pulpit. Charlotte and her children would shiver in their pew, terrified.

(Their father, Winston, felt himself immune from God's judgment: He enjoyed his Sunday mornings getting drunk by himself while Charlotte took the children to church.)

A year ago, Charlotte had gone to Easter Mass at St. James the Less. The new priest was young and adequate, but he shamelessly embraced the festivity of Easter, planning all sorts of graceless activities. On his way out of the church, a young boy smashed right into Charlotte in his hurry to get to the egg hunt in the side yard. "Sorry!" he cried, not stopping.

She yelled "RUDE!" three times, then straightened her blouse, content.

A young mother in a sleeveless Lilly Pulitzer dress furrowed her brow. Her blond hair looked quite attractive pulled back in a low ponytail and tied with a bow. Charlotte nodded at the stylish woman, giving her Louisa's distant smile, but the woman glared back. "Yelling at a kid?" she said.

"He was very rude," noted Charlotte.

"It's Easter," said the woman. "What's wrong with you, lady?"

The woman walked toward the egg hunt and Charlotte was overwhelmed with shame.

Now, sitting in her pew, Charlotte felt her usual unease—plus a sharper kind: maternal fear. What if she could be helping, over there across the ocean? And if she happened into Paros, that would be wonderful, but the point was that Charlotte needed to pack her monogrammed bag and go to her family! As soon as mass was over, Charlotte drove her golf cart home, went straight to her phone book, called Skidaway Travel, and booked herself a flight to Athens, Greece. She tried to reach Lee and Cord, her rich children, to get her an upgrade, but neither answered. Charlotte went ahead and put a ticket she could afford on her AmEx.

Economy class—so gauche!

39 CORD

CORD HAD NO PLAN.

He and Giovanni sat in a circle of fellow phone addicts, each with a leather-bound notebook open on their lap. The facilitator of the "Make a Plan to Stay Screen-Free" workshop played binaural beats over the sound system—gongs and whatnot. Cord's ass ached on the thin yoga mat where he sat cross-legged.

Everyone else, including Gio, scribbled furiously. Cord stared into space, loathing the facilitator, the gongs, the other participants, and most of all, his fiancé.

He wanted to work. He wanted to scroll. He wanted a drink.

"Take a moment to breathe," cooed Ashworth, the facilitator-slash-yoga-teacher. "And now . . . let's begin with you, Cord. What's your plan to stay screen-free?"

Cord didn't answer right away. He flipped his notebook closed and opened it again. The page was still blank. He tried to make his hand move. It didn't.

"I have no plan," said Cord.

Giovanni exhaled dramatically.

"I'm sorry," said Cord. "I don't mean to be impolite. I just don't want to be here. Honestly, I don't have a problem with my phone. I'm just an adult with a job. I *don't have time* to journal. And—to be frank—I *don't want to have time* to journal."

"This is what I'm saying," said Giovanni, turning to the woman seated on his left. Winifred, long-haired and elegant in her fifties, shook her head knowingly. "He doesn't even think it's a problem," confided Gio.

"Then tell me, Giovanni," said Cord, "what is the problem, exactly?"

Giovanni turned toward him. "You're just . . . gone. You're numb. And when you're forced to sit in your feelings, you're a jerk."

Winifred gave a little shrug. "Phil's a jerk without his numbing agents, too."

Balding Phil closed his eyes, a portrait of resigned despair.

Cord stared at Phil, thinking, *Nope. Just no.*

He stood abruptly. "I'm done," said Cord. He picked up his notebook and flung it into the koi pond beside the Event Kottage. Then, with a sigh, he went back and fished it out. "Sorry," he muttered. "Didn't mean to hurt the fish."

As he walked to the parking lot, he heard Giovanni's voice behind him, low and tight with anger—but didn't catch the words. He wasn't sure he wanted to.

Cord climbed into the rental car they'd picked up in town, slammed the door, and turned the key. It would take a few minutes to reach their Kottage, pack his bags, and depart. *Numb*—the word hung in the air like smoke. Cord sat in the driver's seat for a moment longer, notebook dripping in his lap, wondering why he'd rather be numb than feel a thing.

40 LEE

She had to be outside. Still in her nightgown, she pulled on a coat and walked down the stairs, into the Athenian dark. The city felt lush with possibility—something vital was happening. She just had to figure out what it was. Had Regan stepped outside this same door, searching? She had been missing for almost two weeks.

Show me the path, Lee asked her sister.

The moonlight turned everything silver—ancient walls, sleeping cats, closed tavernas. Lee hadn't slept in forty-eight hours but had no fatigue, only a fantastic energy that made her skin vibrate in a weirdly pleasing way. Her mouth was dry, her pulse visible at her wrists. This was what she'd been missing—this electric aliveness.

Lee walked fast, her coat flying open, hair streaming behind her. She was magnificent. She was exactly who she was meant to be—not dulled by medications. This was her true self: wild, intuitive, connected to frequencies others couldn't hear.

The city transformed as she walked along Pireos Street. Modern Athens peeled away like old paint, revealing layers of history.

She reached the ancient cemetery of Kerameikos and jumped its fence, her nightgown catching briefly on a metal spike.

The archaeological site was sacred. Broken marble columns studded the tall grass, and gravestones carved with scenes of farewell shone. A statue of a mourning woman seemed to turn toward her. Lee moved deeper into the ruins, past excavated foundations. The herbal scent of fennel and wild thyme mixed with the dusty smell of ancient marble.

"Regan?" she called softly.

She climbed onto a broken column, standing among relics, feeling holy. Night air filled Lee's lungs, and she spread her arms. The Acropolis glowed in the distance, its clean columns echoing the shattered ones around her.

Lee waited, every nerve lit. Any moment now, Regan would appear—step out from behind a pillar, rise from the marble foundations. They would embrace. Lee would say, *I see the world you see.*

But nothing moved.

Finally, Lee stumbled back to the ground, her foot tearing on a sharp edge of marble. But the pain in her foot was outside of her and she could be outside the pain.

Regan was not here.

Lee scrambled back over the fence. The city hadn't changed. Buses hissed, voices floated from a late-night kiosk. She continued to walk, eventually reaching a massive nightclub housed in a converted mansion. Heavy bass drew her close. She approached the entrance in her torn nightgown and overcoat, foot bleeding. The bouncer looked her up and down.

He stepped aside. Of course he stepped aside.

She was Lee Perkins.

She belonged everywhere.

Lee pushed through the heavy doors into strobing lights, a

crushing crowd, air thick with smoke and sweat and something chemical-sweet. Bodies pressed against her. She moved deeper into the club, hearing a hundred hearts beating, knowing she would find her sister. She would solve everything. She was invincible.

Lee could finally see the secret world.

41 REGAN & FRANÇOIS

My love, I am headed to the airport. I can't believe I will finally see you! This was all so sudden. I wish I could bring the girls.

That will come with time, my love. We need to meet, just you and me. Are you certain you don't need me to pay for the room? I am very frustrated with my accountant.

I have paid. I told the girls I would be gone until Sunday. We will have four days together if all goes well with my flights! The hotel looks beautiful.

It is a special place with wonderful beaches. My colleague has a villa nearby.

I left the note you suggested,
but I'm a little worried. I think
they would have understood if
I had told them I was meeting
you.

Do you want to cancel? If you don't
love me, just tell me now.

No, I don't want to cancel!

Hello?

François?

I'm sorry. You are right, the
girls will be fine. I didn't
tell them anything, I
promise. Please come and
meet me.

François?

I will text as soon as I land. I love
you.

I love you, François.

I cannot wait to hold you in my
arms . . . and more.

Same here!!!!!

My love, there is a problem.

                              François, no.

They are telling me I need to pay
some customs fee for my business
equipment. These officials are
extortionists!

Regan?

Regan?

                              How much do you need?

Five thousand US. They say I can
clear customs as soon as I pay the
fee, my love. I am calling my
accountant, but he says it will take
three days to transfer my money
from my Tether wallet. Tell me
what to do.

                              I don't have anything left until
                              my Kraken Futures account is
                              unfrozen.

I am frustrated beyond words! I
am heartbroken!

                              OK, I will take cash from my
                              BBB account.

This will also take three days. It is
the weekend. I will return to Paris
and we can try to be together at
another time. I am so close, but it
is impossible. I cannot take any
more money from you, my love. As
soon as my accounts are liquid, we
will move forward with our life
together!

How do you want the money?

My Tether wallet will work, but I
cannot ask you for more, Regan!
Where will you find it?

It's done. I will see you soon.

My love, you are magical! I see the
money in my account. I will go now
to clear customs and see you
shortly!

I love you, François. I will be
waiting.

I have landed in Ercan,
François! Are you at the
hotel?

François? I don't think my
messages are going through. I

will drive to the hotel and see
you there!

I have checked into room 402. I
will be waiting for you, my love.

François?

François?

François?

42 LEE

LEE WAS DREAMING OF HER CHILDHOOD GUINEA PIG, LUTHER, WHEN a sharp, repetitive tapping pulled her from her cozy childhood bedroom, which had been wallpapered in blue hearts. When she opened her eyes and found herself in Regan's sparse Greek bedroom, she felt deflated. And Luther—what a cutie he had been, if a bit smelly. He had died of "mysterious causes" soon after Lee went to college.

The tapping continued. "What?" she said, with irritation, "WHAT IS IT?"

The doorknob opened and there was Flora, rendered timid by Lee's loud and angry voice. "Auntie Lee?" said Flora.

"I'm sorry, do you need a ride to school?" Lee sat up—this motherhood shtick never ended. Day after day with the rides to school and the lunch ingredients and the pretending to listen when she just wanted to stare into space, JESUS.

"It's Saturday," said Flora flatly.

"What do you need?" said Lee through clenched teeth. She was honestly finished with these children and their constant maintenance! She was such a bad person! She added, "Sweetheart?"

"There's someone here," said Flora, speaking slowly as if Lee were hard of hearing. "Do you want to get up and come into the living room?"

"Is it your mom?" said Lee.

"Oh no," said Flora, looking sick. "No, it's not Mom."

"Who is it, honey?"

"Come see."

Lee stood grouchily and followed Flora into the living room, where she was stunned to see *her* mother on the couch. "It's me! Surprise!" said Charlotte, jumping up and splaying open her hands.

"Mom!" said Lee, the word coming out strangled. Charlotte wasn't supposed to be here. Lee was supposed to have found Regan by now, supposed to have fixed everything before anyone else needed to get involved. Charlotte's presence meant only one thing: Lee had failed so spectacularly that her elderly mother had flown across an ocean to clean up the mess.

"Sounded like you needed some help around here," said Charlotte, looking pointedly at the living room floor, which was scattered with take-out wrappers and half-folded clothes, and at Isabelle, entwined with Anastasia on the couch.

Flora gazed adoringly at Charlotte, her savior. Charlotte wore a fuchsia pantsuit and leopard-print slingbacks. "Grammy Charlotte," said Flora, "do you want some coffee?"

"That would be delightful," said Charlotte. "And can you move my monogrammed bag into my bedroom? After coffee, let's make a grocery list. You girls need some healthy meals around here, I can see! When did anyone last clean? And Isabelle, dear, why are you and your pal still in pajamas at—good Lord, is it really noon?"

Lee watched Flora's face light up with relief that a real adult had finally arrived. Anastasia, clad in a T-shirt and thong, rose from the couch and headed to Isabelle's room.

"That girl needs *bigger panties!*" whispered Charlotte.

Lee might as well have been furniture.

"Grammy Charlotte, sleep with me!" said Flora.

"Oh, that's sweet," said Charlotte. "But I'll stay in the guest room."

"Um, there is no guest room," said Isabelle, seemingly happy to rain on Charlotte's parade.

"This is an utter disaster," Charlotte muttered.

"You can say that again," said Isabelle.

Lee stood frozen as Charlotte began issuing orders—Flora to the kitchen, Isabelle to get dressed, clean that surface, pull up the *New York Times* cooking app. Within minutes, Charlotte had done what Lee couldn't do in two weeks: made the girls feel safe and cared for.

Lee stood off to the side, arms limp. Her nightgown was torn. Her foot was cut badly. Flora looked at Lee worriedly. Lee didn't blame her.

Lee needed her mother, and here she was.

"Go back to bed, dear," said Charlotte. "You look simply awful."

Lee wanted to protest. She opened her mouth, then closed it. She turned and went back to bed, like a child. For a few more blessed hours, she would remain oblivious to what she had done.

43 LEE

LEE HAD BEEN IGNORING HER PHONE, ROLLING BACK AND FORTH IN Regan's bed, unable to sleep. When she picked up her device, she saw that Francine had called six times . . . and proceeded to call again as Lee stared at the screen. "Hello?" said Lee, her voice hoarse.

"Lee! I'm glad you answered. These photos are *something.*"

"What photos?"

"From . . . Villa Mercedes? You, in a nightgown, looking absolutely—"

Lee sat up, head pounding. Fragments of the night before came back to her—the cemetery, the fence, the club. The glorious feeling that everything made sense, and was snapping effortlessly into place. Lee put Francine on speaker and opened Instagram. There she was inside Villa Mercedes in a ripped nightgown, eyes bright with mania. The comments ranged from concern to mockery to artistic appreciation.

Raw and beautiful
This is what real pain looks like

Lee Perkins serving GLAM even in
crisis
Mental health awareness queen

She was viral again. Not for her talent, not for her work, but
for her public disintegration, packaged and consumed as entertainment.

"Lee?" said Francine. "Are you there? Are you there, Lee?"

44 CORD

CORD CELEBRATED THREE DAYS OF SOBRIETY WITH A GLASS OF GIN at Snug Tavern in Tannersville, New York, followed by two more glasses of gin. After striding out of the journal-writing session, Cord had packed his bags. Giovanni, ever the teacher's pet, had finished the "Make a Plan to Stay Screen-Free" workshop, then jogged back to Kiss Me Kottage #12 in time to inform Cord that if he left the "Return to Love Retreat," he could keep on driving and never come back.

Cord called him a terrorist and took the car.

There had been a proverbial gun on the mantel of their relationship for some time. Both had wanted to ignore it, to keep an explosion at bay. Their relationship had become (to add yet another metaphor . . . or was it a simile?) a poisonous plant that entrapped them both. But as the world changed—first the Covid lockdown and then the confusing aftermath—both Cord and Giovanni found a very real comfort tangled in the vines of their toxic relationship. Now Cord had picked up Chekhov's metaphorical gun, taken aim, and shot. At the metaphorical plant. He had shot his way free, leaving ruin in his wake and his cellphone in a lockbox, in a safe.

Now what?

The bartender at Snug Tavern poured a fourth gin to go, and Cord nestled the plastic cup between his thighs as he drove. Fuck Giovanni and fuck the tyrannical "Return to Love Retreat" and fuck NYC Ventures. None of it had worked—he'd tried it drunk, and he'd tried it sober. For lack of a better idea, Cord punched his mother's address into the rental car GPS: 37 Wiley Bottom Road, Savannah, Georgia.

In thirteen hours and forty-four minutes, he'd be back in his mom's house, the closest thing he had to a home. Charlotte wouldn't judge him for drinking gin and scrolling his phone— once he got a new phone. She would love him joining her in front of the *CBS Evening News*. Maybe at the very site of the childhood that had maimed him, he could find a way to stumble forward. In any case, he could rest. Cord smiled. He could taste the Triscuits and cheddar already.

45 LEE

IN ATHENS, LEE AND CHARLOTTE SHARED REGAN'S ROOM. CHAR-
lotte snored softly, her fragrance—a mixture of Jean Naté bath oil
and a musky scent that was Charlotte's alone—rousing a jumble
of emotions in Lee: security, anxiety, sadness. Charlotte stirred,
rolling away from her daughter.

Lee remembered the sweet shock of waking next to a man.
Back when she had been carefree and wild, there had been naked
Captain Luigi on the *Splendido Marveloso* cruise ship. At the time,
all she had wanted was fame, some sort of validation from the
universe that she was meant to be a star. Jason had just dumped
her, and she felt emancipated. Those were the days when her
mental problems lent her a sort of sparkle.

Ah, Captain Luigi. Too bad he was old, bad in the sack, and
married.

Then Lee had met Kiko, a tour guide and chef on the island of
Malta. She had allowed herself to dream of a life with him, even
considering moving to Valletta, of all places! What if she'd gone
and done it? But the universe had intervened, or God, or just biol-
ogy: She'd tried to jump off her cruise ship balcony; some Peep-
ing Tom had filmed it; and the rest was history. She was now,
officially, famous for being insane.

For wanting someone to love her.

Lee allowed herself a moment to acknowledge that she really *did* want to act again, but in a *real* film, with a prestige director. She wasn't going to have a family of her own. She was never going to bear children. Why not aim to live on through beautiful, important work? Lee vowed to get her prescriptions organized and reach out to Francine. Her brain seemed to have recovered from the last episode, but anything could happen . . . worst of all, a deep depression.

Why did Lee have a sick brain? She tried not to ask this question, but it plagued her. It was scary not to know who you were, not to be able to trust your own thoughts. She was very tired from hanging on, keeping the door closed, staying.

Charlotte turned over, her hands clasped together. She opened her eyes, and Lee noticed that the blue of her irises had paled—was this a thing that happened with age?

"Hi, sweetheart," said Charlotte.

"Hi, Mom."

"I wrote to Paros," said Charlotte. "I made a mistake when I told him I couldn't leave Palmetto Shores."

"Oh! Did he respond?"

"It was an actual letter," said Charlotte, snootily. "He's probably just getting it, or the letter might still be airborne. Above the Med."

Lee smiled. Charlotte loved glamour. "What if he says he still loves you?" she asked.

Charlotte considered. "He's probably dead," she said. She sat up. "And furthermore," she said, her method of ending the discussion. Charlotte changed the subject. "Lee Lee, I am really starting to worry about Regan. What on earth has she gotten herself into?"

"Some sort of money scam, I think," said Lee.

"Do you think she ran off with her new French boyfriend? But that just isn't like her, is it?"

"François isn't real," said Lee. "It's some thief who pretends to be a French boyfriend."

"*Trafficked with Mariana van Zeller* did an episode on this," said Charlotte soberly. "Remember? A woman in Kansas thought she was engaged to a helicopter pilot, but it was a young man in Jordan. Or Jamaica? Maybe Jamaica, Queens . . ."

"I didn't see that episode," said Lee.

"You did, too," said Charlotte. "Who else would I have watched it with?"

There was a quiet moment, as mother and daughter both acknowledged that they only had each other.

Charlotte broke the silence. "And then there was that ugly fat man? Who thought a Brazilian model was in love with him?" Charlotte laughed meanly. "But it was a high school teenager in Texas, using photos from a supermodel's Facebook page! People are stupid."

Lee did not point out that her mother had flown "across the Med" to rekindle a relationship with a man she'd last spoken with ten years before. But was it stupid to dream of being loved? Where was the line between stupidity and hope?

46

LOVE HACKERS
BY FLORA WILLINGHAM

EDDIE, THE YAHOO BOY

The Yahoo Boy says his real name is Eddie and he is twelve years old. He wears a sleeveless T-shirt and shorts. He tells me he is barefoot, although I can't see his feet on WhatsApp. I found Eddie after responding to his WhatsApp message attempting to "pig butcher" me.

(The message said, *Susie, is this your number?* I responded, *No but I will pay you $50 USD in Tether to chat right now for ten minutes.* To my shock, he called me immediately. I was very happy to have a **primary source** #1.)

When Eddie calls me, he is in his brother's hair salon. On his phone camera, he shows me around King Salon, a wooden building on stilts, situated, he says, "in the biggest floating slum in the world." I ask him where exactly and he says, "Nigeria, man, what do you think?"

Eddie's brother, who goes by "King," has booted up his generator and Eddie and a dozen kids are charging their cellphones while we talk. They yell and wave in the background.

"If you have a phone, you have a chance," Eddie says.

To be honest, I admire them. Eddie says they sit in King Salon and text all day. When I ask how many texts he sends daily, Eddie says, "At least five hundred or more, like one thousand."

He notes, "If one person texts back, it is gold."

I ask Eddie if he remembers any women from Savannah, Georgia; if he remembers *anyone* specifically; if he remembers anyone with my mom's name, Regan Willingham. It's possible, isn't it, that little Eddie could be François?

Eddie says, "I remember nobody and nothing."

If he gets a "customer," he sends them up the chain. He is just the **Bomber,** using the few English-language scripts he's been able to buy. If someone responds, **Editors** get involved, then **Loaders, Pickers, Billers,** and—in the worst-case scenarios—**Yahoo Plus** or **Yahoo Plus Plus,** but this is less common now that the murders in the city have come to light.

Eddie says he scams to get money for school tuition and the required uniform. He hopes to be a barber like his brother someday, and when that day comes, he and his brother will rename the building "Two Kings Salon."

47 CORD

CORD COULD NOT CONVINCE THE WOMAN AT THE GUARDHOUSE TO let him into Palmetto Shores, his mother's gated community on an island off the coast of Savannah. "My mom *lives* here," he said. "Her name is Charlotte Perkins! 37 Wiley Bottom Road."

"Honey, I'm not saying I don't believe you. But she didn't call you in a pass." The guard was bored and her fingernails were ruby talons with diamond chips.

"I love your nails," said Cord.

"Appreciate you," said the woman.

"You know what?" said Cord. "I'm trying to surprise my mom for her birthday."

"I see you're getting that party started," said the guard, staring pointedly at the can of beer in Cord's crotch.

"I don't have a phone to call her," said Cord. "Can I use yours?"

"I just told you, honey: She's not answering her phone." Cord loved this woman's accent. He was unreasonably gleeful to be back in Georgia. "Listen. I can park in the public lot and walk all the way to Wiley Bottom Road," said Cord, "or you can let me in."

"I sure am sorry, honey. You have a good one, now," said the woman. Cord gritted his teeth, reversed loudly, then spun around to park outside Publix, a grocery store that had five times the amount of fried chicken parts for sale as his Manhattan grocery store, which almost begrudgingly offered only organic, flash-frozen tenders. Cord left his suitcase in the car, grabbed two beers, and began to walk, taking the forested golf cart path that skirted the guardhouse.

The Savannah night was pleasant. Cord hadn't seen his mom in a long time. He knew he had to quit booze again; he knew he would. He'd have to go to all the goddamn meetings, recite all the platitudes. He could skip Step One—he understood his life was unmanageable. It was always Step Two that tripped him up. Why, oh, why couldn't he accept that there was a *power greater than himself*?

Cord believed, at his core, that if he didn't handle everything, from the Sweethearts IPO to paying the bills to working out at precisely every morning at six A.M., he—and those he loved—would be fucked. And he had turned out to be right—here he was *like a cat burglar* breaking into his mother's gated community, drunk and dumped. And probably fired, though he wasn't sure if he could be fired—but he guessed he was about to find out.

Cord had once had an Alcoholics Anonymous sponsor, Handy, who had tried very hard to help him. And it wasn't—*it was not*—that Cord thought he was better than Handy (he obviously *wasn't* better than Handy, who had been sober for decades), but he found himself dreading the potlucks at Handy's house, the AA meetings, the coffee klatches, the imperative to respond all the time when Handy texted, hey buddy, checking in.

Cord stopped "checking in" around the first two weeks of lockdown. He instacarted a very good bottle of Sangiovese about two weeks after that.

What Cord wanted was a third avenue: not to drink too much,

but not to have to put in all the unrelenting work of sobriety. He wanted to be like Charlotte: easy, breezy, beautiful.

Maybe he should make a "Sweethearts" app, but for AA sponsors. Could a chatbot keep him sober without all the muss and fuss of human connection?

As he traversed Tidewater Square to Brandenberry Road, Cord smelled pine needles. On his left was a body of water he didn't know the name of (or maybe it was a marsh? Lagoon?) and a house some rich guy had built to withstand hurricanes (good luck with that). The hurricane house was a normal house elevated by concrete piers. *We're all trying to game disaster,* thought Cord.

Finally, he reached his mom's yard. It was a bit overgrown but Cord loved every inch: the live oaks draped in Spanish moss, the palmetto palms, and Charlotte's pink azaleas. But there was something new poking out from beside Cord's mother's front door . . . and it was a flagpole. Cord put his hand on his chest. Had Charlotte become an old woman who hung seasonal flags? It seemed that yes, she had. A flag featuring the deranged face of an Easter bunny (poor bunny, those teeth!) hung limply in the humid evening. Gauche!

Cord trudged along the brick driveway to the front door, which was locked. Luckily, he knew the garage code. (It was his birthday.) He maneuvered his way past the golf cart in the dark, grabbed a dusty bottle of champagne from his mom's wine fridge, and let himself into the kitchen.

"Yoo-hoo!" called Cord.

There was no answer, and the house was completely dark.

48 LEE

CHARLOTTE TOOK CHARGE. SHE DROVE THE GIRLS TO SCHOOL, SHOPPED in the local markets, made scrumptious dinners, and cleaned the kitchen. Lee's job was not killing herself and taking out the trash. As Lee pushed open the door, garbage in hand, the big Samoyed stray dog would appear from behind a hedge, looking away from Lee as if to convey indifference. Lee decided to name the dog Yassus, then bought a bag of dog food, bowl, and sealed container to keep in the vestibule of Regan's building. Every morning and evening, Lee left food for Yassus, who waited for Lee to avert her gaze, then lunged at the bowl. She appreciated the dog's desire to feign nonchalance.

No one talked about Regan.

Flora found a way to get Charlotte's beloved *New York Times* delivered and Charlotte completed the morning crossword, asking for everyone's help when needed. Flora called for takeout when her grandmother wanted "to put her feet up." Even the Greek deli owner knew their usual now—spanakopita for Charlotte, moussaka for Lee, vegetarian dolmades for the girls. "Same as always?" he'd ask, and Lee would nod, surprised they had an "always." Three generations of women existing in a bubble—it couldn't go on, and yet it did: dinners and dishes and finishing bottle after bottle of wine and taking out the trash, Lee feeling a rare flash of joy when Yassus appeared for his supper.

After many, many calls, Lee located an English-speaking doctor who could see her on short notice. She booked his first-available appointment, vowing to return her agent's many messages as soon as she was properly medicated. Lee's meeting with the doctor was short and sweet; he called her prescriptions in to a pharmacy that would have them ready the following morning.

After seeing the psychiatrist, Lee offered to gather the girls at their posh school, the afternoon sun low in the sky. While both girls were comfortable taking the metro, they preferred an air-conditioned ride—when Lee texted to ask if they'd like a pickup, Flora sent a thumbs-up emoji.

Lee eased her rental car through the ornate wrought-iron gates, a crushed gravel driveway crunching beneath her tires as the imposing main building came into full view—a weathered limestone façade with classical columns and ivy climbing up the walls. A central clock tower dominated the symmetrical wings, and immaculate stonework was adorned with crests and decorative friezes. If the founders of the American School of Athens had meant to create a campus that evoked a New England boarding school—or Harvard—they had succeeded.

Lee entered a long line of cars piloted by well-coiffed women. On the radio, she found her anthem: "Girls Just Want to Have Fun," by Cyndi Lauper. She rolled down the window to sing along: *Phone rings, in the middle of the night, my faaaa-ther yells, "what you going to do with your life?"*

Flora stood alone in front of the school, somber in her uniform. Lee waved as she pulled up. Flora climbed in. "Where's Isabelle?" said Lee.

"I don't know," said Flora. Lee turned right out of the school driveway, accelerating maybe too fast but not so fast that she deserved the crossing guard's glare and whistle. "Fuck off!" Lee yelled at the crossing guard, feeling feisty.

Flora's brow furrowed.

"Should I wait for Isabelle?" said Lee. "Well, never mind, too late! You snooze, you lose. Am I right, Flora?" Lee's heart seemed to be racing, and she felt very *glad* all of a sudden—glad to be in Athens, glad to be the sort of person who picked up her sweet, sorrowful niece from school.

"I miss Mom," said Flora.

Lee's phone rang: Francine. "Sorry, sweetheart," said Lee. "I've been avoiding my agent—this will be quick." She put the phone on speaker. "Hi, Francine," she said.

"Lee," said Francine. "Why haven't you called me back? I've been trying and trying! You're *still trending*. You in that nightgown, you're everywhere—TikTok, TMZ, gossip mags . . . and wait until you hear this, Lee! Are you ready, Lee? Are you ready?"

In the rearview mirror, Flora seemed forlorn, looking out of the window at the gridlocked Athens traffic. She turned to face Lee. "Auntie Lee?" she said.

"One second, Flora."

"Are you ready?" cried Francine.

"I am ready," said Lee.

"Lee Perkins, I've had a call from Ben Morris. *BEN MORRIS!* He wants you to read for his new film! This is the role of a lifetime, Lee!"

"Wait, opposite Jason?"

"Yes! Jason is confirmed for Lord Byron and they want you to read for Lady Caroline Lamb, his wild and wacky lover or something. I'll set the call. OK?"

Lee was filled with euphoria. At last! Lee *knew* she'd eventually be seen for the generational talent she was . . . and now it was actually happening. But she wanted to hide her joy from sad little

Flora—it was inappropriate to feel proud and thrilled while Regan was still missing. "Francine . . ." said Lee, eyeing her niece in the back seat.

"I know, I know, the timing is appalling! But I'll set the call, Lee. You *have* to take this call. You have to! And, oh, sorry—are you OK? Any word on your sister?"

"No," said Lee. "No word."

"Christ. And how are you . . . mentally?"

"Everything's under control."

"I'm glad. I'm very glad, honey. Ben said the photos are exactly what he's been looking for. Raw. Real. 'Authentic trauma,' he called it—he says you're *perfect* for Lady Caroline—'a gorgeous woman, unraveling in public, beautiful in her destruction.' His exact words, Lee!"

"Wow," said Lee, her good mood making it easier than usual to ignore the fact that yet another man in Hollywood thought Lee's breakdown was more interesting than her acting abilities.

"Ciao bella! Or should I say . . . what the hell do the Greeks say for adios?"

"Antío," muttered Flora.

"They say 'an-dee-oh,' " said Lee.

"Well, whatever," said Francine, ending the call.

"An-dee-oh," repeated Lee, dreamily.

Flora was still glaring at her. Lee wrenched her gaze from the rearview mirror. Her niece was needing something, asking for something, and Lee was—like all the other adults in Flora's life—letting her down. "Flora," said Lee, her buoyant frame of mind startlingly unaffected by Flora's misery. "Did you hear what Francine said?"

"Yeah, I heard," scoffed Flora, looking at her hands.

Lee swerved and zipped through Athens traffic as if she were being guided. Lee was going to pull this off—all of it! She was meant to be famous again. She would win an Academy Award! And she would find Regan. "Obviously, I'm not going anywhere until we find your mom," noted Lee.

"Sure," muttered Flora.

Lee literally couldn't bear to look at her niece. She had left her little brother and sister in Savannah to become famous, and she was going to leave this girl, too. But what else was she supposed to do?

Lee parked in Regan's driveway. Inside, she paced the length of the apartment and then went into the cramped kitchen and pushed the button to raise the metal shades. She found a very small apple and sliced it into perfect, symmetrical wedges. She spooned some grainy Greek peanut butter onto the plate and drizzled it with honey, then brought the plate to her niece.

Flora looked up from her computer. She had changed from her uniform into shorts and the faded pink T-shirt. "What is this?" she said.

"An after-school snack," said Lee brightly. Lee perched on Flora's bed. She took an apple slice and munched. "I'm calling Markos every day," she said. "He's committed to finding your mom, Flora, and I am too."

Flora's fingers paused on her keyboard. She turned slowly, something hard in her expression. "Really?" She gestured to her screen. "Then what's this?"

Lee stood and crossed to look at the computer, where she saw a photo of herself and Markos, walking in Anafiotika. The gossip website or whatever it was had made a video close-up of Lee's hand holding Markos's hand. The headline read:

MY BIG FAT GREEK POLICE OFFICER!
Lee Perkins's Mystery Lover REVEALED: He's a COP!

"Oh no," said Lee.

"Why would you get involved with the man trying to find Mom?" said Flora. "It's just like Mom always said—you only care about yourself!"

The words hit Lee like a slap, though the accusation was one Regan had lobbed at her countless times . . . during late-night phone calls when Regan caught her not really listening (she was scrolling Instagram); when Lee had cut visits home short for auditions; the day, long ago, when Lee had ditched her younger siblings to escape to California.

"Flora, no," said Lee. But even as she denied it, she wondered: Was she here to save Regan, or to play the role of saving Regan?

"Can you please get out of my room?" said Flora.

"Wait," said Lee. Her mind spun.

"GET OUT OF MY ROOM!" yelled Flora.

"I need my medication refills," said Lee.

"Then get your refills!" said Flora. "You're an adult!" She wheeled her chair back around to her computer, using the back of her hand to wipe tears from her cheeks.

You hurt everyone you love, said Depression.

The front door of the apartment banged open. "Yoo-hoo!" called Charlotte.

Flora stood and ran away from Lee, to her grandmother.

49 CHARLOTTE

CHARLOTTE SIPPED HER COFFEE. IT WAS NICE TO FEEL NEEDED IN Athens, Greece, though at times she felt as if she was running a two-star bed-and-breakfast, just cooking and cleaning like a scullery maid. With the girls situated at their fancy school and Lee sleeping late (as usual), Charlotte was at loose ends. She decided to head to the local market, which was more like a Gas Mart than a real store. No grocery carts! Brown eggs with bits of straw and feathers clinging to them! Charlotte bought a dozen, and, as usual, the shopkeeper wrapped the eggs in dirty newspaper.

There was no actual fresh milk, just some foil-box "long-life" milk, which tasted downright weird. No sliced cheddar, just icebergs of feta floating in oceanic brine, scooped out by hand. Instead of an appealing wheel of Brie, Charlotte sampled hard cheeses called graviera, kasseri, and kefalotyri. They were revolting, too salty; the word that came to mind was "fetid."

The butcher shop down the street reeked and featured hanging legs of spiced beef and air-dried pork. When Charlotte asked for thin-sliced honey ham—her preference for a sandwich—the fat man with blood on his apron told her they only sold "full cuts, real meat, like for boiling." Beneath the fatty bits of meat, Charlotte spied an ashtray with a half-smoked cigarette. She supposed she should have been glad he put his cigarette out to serve her!

And woe to the American who yearned for a bag of uniformly sliced sandwich bread! There were none of the snacks that made packing lunches simple, the Go-Gurts and Fruit Roll-Ups, the cute and salty Goldfish crackers. Charlotte could not bring herself to buy dried prunes. She got the weensy bags of potato chips, and—for dinner—fresh pasta, a can (not a bottle) of olive oil, lemons with the leaves attached.

No Mallomars! Charlotte bought some cheap-looking cookies called Gemista.

After unpacking her groceries mid-morning, Charlotte ran out of things to do. Outside seemed overwhelming, but not going out felt worse. She put on her sunglasses and a floppy hat that read IT'S ALL GREEK TO ME, and walked.

She checked her phone for messages. Paros still hadn't called.

At last, she reached the Acropolis Museum, a sleek monument of glass and steel. Blessedly cool inside, the museum floated above an ancient excavation site. Charlotte saw broken walls and sunken hearths beneath the glass floor. People had lived here thousands of years ago.

She wandered through the Archaic Gallery. Blank-eyed statues stared into eternity. She picked up a magnifier and peered through it to see fossilized seashells embedded in the marble. Charlotte tried to feel enchanted.

The glorious Parthenon Gallery had been designed to mirror the exact dimensions and orientation of the temple itself. Through wall-to-ceiling windows, Charlotte watched the merciless sun beat down on the actual Parthenon. A tour guide spoke loudly in English behind her. "Behold the Parthenon temple, dedicated to the goddess Athena. It is two thousand four hundred and seventy years young," he boomed. "The Elgin Marbles were hacksawed off and stolen in the nineteenth century. Their spaces remain, waiting for them to be returned."

Charlotte pretended she wasn't eavesdropping.

"We have created blank spaces for the stolen Elgin Marbles to live when they are returned. More and more museums are researching the provenance of their heists."

The guide walked to a corner and pointed to a red dot on the floor. "This dot," he exclaimed, "marks the exact spot where an ancient craftsman once dropped a tool while working on the original temple."

Charlotte stared at the dot, realizing with sadness that she'd never understood Paros, who had tried to explain where he belonged. She had treated Paros like a souvenir . . . like something she could cut from his world, bring home to hers. Maybe that was why he hadn't called.

The guide went on. "Now," he said, "this mistake will be remembered for all time."

Isn't that always the way with mistakes, thought Charlotte.

LOVE HACKERS
BY FLORA WILLINGHAM

SÈMÈGÀN, YAHOO PLUS PLUS

Eddie contacted me a few weeks after our interview on WhatsApp. He told me that for $100 USD in Tether, his cousin (who was a prison guard) could connect me to a scammer who was in jail for something known as "Yahoo Plus Plus." With the assistance of a generous friend named Anastasia Boosalis, I was able to send the Bitcoin. Below is my **primary source** #2.

Sèmègàn is in jail, serving a life sentence for murder. His crime is killing a young woman as part of a ritual to enhance his success in online scams. Sèmègàn's story is a chilling example of the extreme lengths some scammers are willing to go to in order to achieve their goals. Known as "Yahoo Plus Plus," this dark variant of the traditional "Yahoo Boys" scam involves the use of human sacrifices and black magic to increase the chances of success.

Sèmègàn explains that he was introduced to the world of online scams by his friends, who taught him how to create fake profiles and manipulate victims. But as the competition grew fiercer, Sèmègàn turned to more extreme measures.

"My brother told me about a witch doctor who could help me get rich," Sèmègàn says. "The Ifá priest said I needed to make a sacrifice. I didn't want to do it, but I was desperate."

The witch doctor instructed Sèmègàn to bring him the left breast of a young woman, which would be used in a potion to enhance his scamming abilities. Sèmègàn lured a nineteen-year-old girl to a remote location, where he drugged her and carried out the gruesome act.

"I didn't want to kill her," Sèmègàn says, "but I thought it was the only way to escape poverty." His voice is very straightforward, almost emotionless. I know from an episode of *Law & Order: Special Victims Unit* that a "flat affect" can be a result of PTSD.

Believe it or not, Sèmègàn's story is not unique. In recent years, there has been a rise in the number of "Yahoo Plus Plus" cases in Nigeria, with scammers resorting to increasingly violent methods to achieve their goals. The Nigerian government has cracked down on these crimes, but the lure of quick wealth continues to draw young people into the dark world of cyber-spiritualism.

When the WhatsApp chat is over, I can't help but feel really sad. For every scammer like Sèmègàn who is caught, there are many others committing violence and fraud, driven by a desperate desire to escape their circumstances and willing to believe anything.

51 LEE

THE DAYS BEGAN TO BLUR TOGETHER. LEE TOOK HER MEDS. SHE FED the dog.

Late one night, Lee padded to the kitchen for water and found Flora, surrounded by papers, wearing headphones and taking notes on a YouTube video. "Flora, what are you doing?" Lee asked.

She slid her headphones off. "Homework," she said.

"What's that video?" Lee peered at the screen. *"Confessions of a Yahoo Boy?"*

Flora flushed, embarrassed but also defiant. "It's for a school project. It's none of your business, Auntie Lee."

Lee felt helpless—was this really a school project, or was Flora the only one who still believed they would find Regan? How long could her sister's absence go on? "It's late. You should go to bed, Flora."

"No," said Flora, turning back to her computer. Lee didn't know what to say. She filled a glass with water and left Flora to her whirring brain.

52 CORD

CORD DRANK HIS WAY THROUGH HIS MOTHER'S CHARDONNAY, WHICH took a while. He ate all the food in her freezer, cheffing up frozen shrimp with spaghetti and scarfing pizzas and Klondike bars, then mini-muffins from the pantry. He'd been a regimented machine for years, and damn, it felt good to eat crap and lie around.

But where was Charlotte? Her Volkswagen Jetta, freshly washed, remained in the garage. Cord called his mom's cell from her home phone and when she didn't answer, Cord figured she was visiting old friends in Florida or on Hilton Head Island and would be back soon. It was definitely odd, but the more he drank, the less he worried about his mom . . . and about everything.

It was wonderful to be alone. He donned one of Charlotte's monogrammed bathrobes, borrowed her 9 iron and putter (with a monogrammed head cover of course) and as soon as it was too dark to be seen, played Palmetto three, par three, which was located outside Charlotte's sliding glass door. Under the Savannah moon, he lay down flat on the course, wishing he had a cigarette.

Nobody needed him and nobody knew where to find him even if they did need him. Cord watched HGTV and the History Channel and every episode of *Keeping Up with the Kardashians*.

Eventually, however, all good things come to an end . . . and so did Charlotte's wine stash.

Cord drained the final sip in her queenly bed, his head propped up on her tasseled yellow pillows. He sauntered into the living room, pausing to gaze at the family portrait, which had been painted sometime in the early eighties. There he was on canvas—just a boy—just a boy. Just a boy dressed in a tiny white polo shirt and seersucker shorts.

Cord in the painting gazed directly at the viewer of the painting (also Cord). A little Mona Lisa he'd been, his expression inscrutable. *Jesus,* thought Cord, *I was a Pro-Level Disassociator even then.*

Cord had never really felt like a child, because he lived in terror of Winston, his father. His friend Miles had a Sit'n Spin toy in his front hallway and whenever Cord visited he would spin and spin because nobody was going to scream at him while he was at Miles's house. It was absolutely glorious, just twirling faster and faster. Sometimes he even let out a "wooo-hooo!"

But he always had to go home.

What happened to that boy on the Sit'n Spin? Cord had squashed him flat, made him into a man who was just a scam. Cord was a helpful and smart person. He was a man everyone admired and depended on. But he was also someone who needed booze or Instagram reels (or booze *and* Instagram reels) to maintain his perfect façade.

Cord the construct was as false as a Sweethearts chatbot husband, nothing more than an algorithm of trauma who just wanted to whirl around on a fucking Sit'n Spin. Did they even make Sit'n Spins anymore?

In the kitchen fridge, Cord located three St. Pauli Girl beers. (Charlotte believed that men liked beer; she always kept a few on hand.) Cord cracked one open and traversed the carpeted staircase to his mother's "bonus room," still filled with baby toys and a tiny wooden kitchen from when Regan's girls were young. Cord sat cross-legged on the floor of the bonus room, checking out the bookshelves, which were filled with his books from high school and college: *A Box of Rain: Lyrics,* the lyrics of the Grateful Dead; *Gorilla, My Love* by Toni Cade Bambara; *A Separate Peace. The Hobbit*—Christ, he had hated *The Hobbit.* He had hated *The Hobbit* very much! (Was that a gay thing? He'd have to ask around. Cord had certainly been the only boy at Savannah Country Day who'd preferred *Pride and Prejudice* to *The Hobbit.*)

And then there were the photo albums, bindings cracked at the edges. He opened one, remembering peeling back the clear sheet, carefully pressing these photos to the sticky page and smoothing the film back over them. It was a lost world—the time when they'd had to wait after taking a photo to finish the roll; bring it to Bay Camera Company for developing; pick up the photos a week later in their orange-and-white paper envelope, the shiny strips of negatives included. They'd sprawl on their stomachs, peeking through magical images, choosing the memories to preserve.

The album Cord held now, navy blue with the Savannah Country Day School crest, was made when he was still trying desperately to present as straight. He'd inserted photos of himself in his lacrosse uniform, mugging with girls. He'd tried to squish in his boutonniere, but it was just a moldy biohazard now.

Cord analyzed the photos, sipping his St. Pauli Girl. There was his dad, Winston, always a mean, lost look in his eyes. Cord obviously knew that *he* was not the reason his dad killed himself, but Cord also knew he'd been a disappointment, if only because Winston seemed to require *more* in his life, something to keep him bound to the world. And a son utterly lacking in athletic and social skills was not going to be that tethering cord. For a long time, Cord's father and Lee had had a mutual admiration society, but she had grown out of their overly close relationship. Winston had been cruel; knew just what to say to pierce you. He seemed to get off on causing pain. Sometimes, things would be perfectly fine and he'd just start a fight for no reason, as if peacefulness was too uncomfortable for him to bear.

Cord sighed. Everyone had their neural kinks, he supposed. It was ironic that now he had a team of researchers exploiting people's dopamine pathways to keep them addicted to their apps. Back in the day, Winston had only felt sadness, and had somehow known—even if subconsciously—that inflicting pain on his family made *him* feel better. What if Cord's father had had Instagram reels to scroll through? Might endless videos of machinery at work and adorable puppies—these two subjects dominated the content of Cord's reels—have saved Winston?

Charlotte was young in the pictures. And there was Cord's baby sister, Regan, so young when he was in high school. Cord noticed, unnervingly, that in every single image, Regan gazed at her big brother adoringly.

Why did this bother him? He felt, actually, kind of dizzy. Cord sprawled on the old carpet of the bonus room, the floor his nieces had crawled across, his eyes level with all the crap they'd dropped behind their play kitchen: an old sock, a juice box, some plastic toy from a McDonald's Happy Meal.

Memories ran over him like warm water and also like a Mack truck: Snuggling with Regan and reading her books, her face pudgy and trusting. Telling Regan about his day as she listened intently, fascinated by his every observation. During his lacrosse games (he sucked), if he ever looked over his shoulder, he would see little Regan shouting on the sidelines . . . clapping, jumping up and down—all for him.

And he'd been a great fucking brother. He sat and made collages with her, cutting up their mother's fashion magazines. He protected her from Winston and then from Charlotte's neediness. They were siblings and best friends; that was the reality. But then the narrative changed.

When she was in high school, Regan was preyed upon by their skeevy art teacher. Cord hadn't known, hadn't seen it, and hadn't protected her from Mr. Ragdale. Even when she was home from the motel where he had taken her, forever changed but alive, Cord had distanced himself from Regan. She reminded him of how badly he had let her down, their story now one that made Cord hate himself: He had failed his little sister.

Yes. He had. They all had.

But he had also made Regan happy. This was clear in the photos, undeniable. There they were at Cord's graduation, smiling: Regan, Lee, Charlotte. His memories had excised any pleasure, but (and maybe it was the beer) he now remembered that he had loved being Regan's big brother. It was maybe the last part of himself that he had loved.

53 LEE

LEE TOOK HER ZOOM MEETING WITH BEN MORRIS AND HER EX-LOVE Jason from a patio table at a taverna near Regan's apartment. She'd fed Yassus early that morning, noticed his ribs were less prominent. He'd actually wagged his tail when he saw her— a first.

Ben wore his long hair in two braids and appeared to be sitting in a dim cave. Lee had never met Ben in person but loved his work—he'd directed two actors to Academy Award nominations, though neither had won.

Jason looked amazing, if a bit plastic—his forehead was very shiny. He sat at a desk in front of a movie poster: Brad Pitt in *Fight Club*. *Subtle*, thought Lee. She still wanted to kiss him—his lips were even plumper than when he'd been hers.

"I'll be honest, Lee," said Ben, "I didn't know your oeuvre . . . until Jason told me about your press conference. And, of course, the photos in Villa Mercedes."

"Is there any news about Regan, Lee Lee?" said Jason, using his old nickname for her. He was so fake! His concern was obviously an act, but Lee was as trained as he: She simply shook her head, looking sorrowful, and ran her fingertips down her neck to her beautiful collarbones.

"No news," she breathed, looking at the men through her eyelashes.

"I'm sorry," said Ben, transfixed.

Morning sunlight, falling through a vine-covered outdoor canopy, made patterns on Lee's table. The waitress, an older Greek woman, returned with her order: sesame-covered bread rings and honey-soaked donuts with a cold frappé.

"Lee," said Ben. "I'm sorry to be meeting during this difficult time in your life. I can't even fathom what a nightmare you're inside right now, with your sister missing. I just wanted you to know that I've been searching for my Lady Caroline Lamb for six months. *Mad, Bad, and Dangerous to Know* is about Lord Byron, but Lady Caroline was his most important lover, arguably more pivotal to his development than his wife."

"Really?" said Lee, playing the naïf. It was familiar, this sense of determining who she should become and executing the role. She had missed this. Being yourself was awful.

"Ariana Grande is in final talks for Lady Byron," Jason chimed in.

"Wow," said Lee, impressed.

"Lady Caroline was a wealthy socialite," Ben continued. "She was stunningly beautiful, infamous, and daring. If women weren't allowed at a party, she dressed as a male page and snuck in. She was older than Byron—she became a novelist in her own right. Byron was obsessed with her. They wrote each other very erotic love letters. Like, look—" He riffled through a small notebook, found the page, and quoted Byron: "Then your heart . . . what a little volcano! That pours lava through your veins."

"'Lava through your veins,'" said Jason, reverentially. "Lee, you *are* like a volcano, to be honest," he added.

"They sent each other . . ." Ben stopped, his face reddening. He swallowed, then said, "They sent each other pubic hair clippings."

Lee raised her eyebrows.

"Lee, I have auditioned every single actress in Hollywood and some in London," Ben barreled on. "You *are* Lady Caroline Lamb. Here . . . look at her," said Ben, holding a full-color image of a portrait in front of his camera, mercifully turning on a light. The picture showed a woman in a richly detailed page's outfit, complete with a velvet doublet and breeches. Lady Caroline wore a small feathered cap, curls escaping and framing her face. She looked self-assured, fully aware of her scandalous nature and proud of it.

"Oh," said Lee.

Jason made a happy *hmmm* sound in the back of his throat. Lee couldn't tear her eyes away from Lady Caroline's face. That expression, how daring!

She picked up a warm, crusty koulouri and took a bite, followed by a mouthful of a loukoumades donut. At the table next to her, two old men argued. One, dressed in a worn, gray sweater and a flat cap, gestured animatedly with calloused hands as he spoke, a half-empty cup of strong Greek coffee before him.

"Those photos from the nightclub . . . the authenticity of them, your raw beauty—that's exactly what I need for this film."

"I was in a manic state, Ben . . . I'm back on my medications now."

"Yes, I know," said Ben.

"And that is great," said Jason the Sycophant. "Mental health is *so* important," he added.

"I wasn't performing—"

"That's what makes you powerful!" Ben leaned in. "No artifice, no Hollywood polish. Just pure, unfiltered emotion!"

Lee stared at Ben. "You're saying you want to cast me because I had a public breakdown?"

"I'm saying I want to cast you because you're willing to go to places other actresses won't go. Lady Caroline was notorious for her public scenes, her beautiful madness. You understand that from the inside."

"I don't—"

"The vulnerability, Lee. The way you looked lost but luminous at the same time in those tabloid shots. That's what I want to capture on film. That's what's going to win you an Oscar."

Lee wanted an Oscar. Oh, how she wanted an Oscar. "What if I can't access that . . . anymore?" she said softly.

"You can. I can get you there."

Lee looked again at the portrait of Lady Caroline, lit up by passion and probably mania.

"Lee," said Ben, "will you be my Lady Caroline?"

"Say yes, Lee Lee," said Jason.

Lee inhaled. She wanted this. "Call Francine," said Lee.

That night, back at Regan's apartment, Lee lay awake listening to sirens in the distance. She thought about Lady Caroline Lamb, a mental wreck, desperate for attention. Perfect casting, really. Ben Morris had seen exactly who she was.

Francine had called her with an offer that should have changed everything. But in the dark, Lee felt blue and alone. She went to count her sleeping pills—the Greek physician had given her a full month's worth—but she didn't take one.

She wanted to have them all if she needed them all.

54

DEADLINE ONLINE EXCLUSIVE

Lee Perkins in Talks to Play Lady Caroline Lamb in Ben Morris's
"Mad, Bad, and Dangerous to Know"

By Tina Donahoo

EXCLUSIVE: Rising star Lee Perkins (*One of You to Love Me*) is in talks to play the fiery Lady Caroline Lamb in Ben Morris's highly anticipated biopic *Mad, Bad, and Dangerous to Know*. The film, which will star Jason O'Brien as Lord Byron, is already shaping up to be one of the most talked-about projects of the year.

Lady Caroline Lamb, infamous for her torrid affair with Byron and her iconic description of him as "mad, bad, and dangerous to know," is a central figure in the poet's tumultuous life. Her own struggles with what many historians now identify as manic depression (bipolar disorder) make her a deeply complex character. The film will explore the volatile relationship between Byron and Lady Caroline, delving into their passionate but destructive love affair, and how their shared battles with mental illness influenced their lives and legacies.

"Lee brings a raw intensity and vulnerability that perfectly captures the spirit of Lady Caroline," said Morris. "Her ability to embody the duality of strength and fragility makes her the ideal choice for this role."

Morris's agent, Marlowe McKay, has confirmed that Perkins is considering the role. Perkins and her agent, Francine Bloom, could not be reached for comment.

This role would mark a major comeback for Perkins, who rose to fame as the star of the hit reality show *One of You to Love Me*. Recently, she made headlines after a press conference in Athens, Greece, where her younger sister is being investigated as a missing person. The incident brought attention to Perkins's personal struggles, including the immense pressure of life in the public eye and the emotional toll of her family crisis.

An anonymous source, who claims to be a close friend of Perkins, expressed her excitement about Perkins taking on such a layered character. "Lady Caroline was a woman ahead of her time, unafraid to live and love passionately despite the constraints of her era. Her experience with bipolar disorder, much like Byron's, shaped her actions and her creative expression in ways that are both tragic and inspiring."

Production for *Mad, Bad, and Dangerous to Know* begins this summer. The film, written by Pulitzer Prize winner Chari Adora, promises to offer a poignant look at the intersection of genius, mental illness, and the societal pressures faced by two of history's most compelling figures.

Bennigson Productions is behind the project, with producers Theodore Harrison and Trevor Brooks steering the ship toward an awards season release in 2027. Fans can expect a deep dive into the emotional and psychological landscapes of both Byron and Lady Caroline, shedding light on the often misunderstood connection between artistic brilliance and mental illness.

55 LEE

IT WAS STORMING OUTSIDE, THUNDER ROLLING THROUGH PERIODI-
cally. Flora was hunched over the kitchen table. "Quite a deluge,"
said Lee.

"Everyone still talks about Cyclone Athena. It happened before we moved here. The streets turned into rivers and people
were trapped in elevators."

"Jeez," said Lee.

"You were in, like, a mental hospital, right?"

The question took Lee by surprise, but she decided to be honest. "Yes," she said.

"Why?"

It was a relief for Lee to speak openly. "I have a mood regulation disorder," she said. "Do you know what that means?"

"I guess, but nobody really understands brains and how they
work."

Lee snorted, finishing off a mug she'd filled with wine. She
pulled out a chair to join Flora. It was strangely soothing in the
dim kitchen with the rain pounding the streets outside. "More
homework?" she said, gesturing to Flora's notebooks and text-
books.

"First Year Lyceum project," said Flora. "That's what they call tenth grade here." Flora turned her laptop screen toward Lee. "I'm writing about romance scammers."

"Oh . . ."

"I knew Mom was in trouble before she went away," said Flora. "But nobody listened to me." Lee recognized the hurt in Flora's voice—the particular sting of having your observations dismissed. "Isabelle told me to get a life, and Mom told me she was fine," said Flora. "People don't like it when you watch them."

"I know," said Lee. She thought about all the times she'd picked up on subtle cues on set—an actor's insecurity, a director's doubt—and how mentioning these observations had labeled her "difficult" or "too intense."

"I knew my dad was planning to kill himself before he did it," said Lee. She felt immediately nervous—what the hell was she doing telling a kid a thing like this? But Charlotte never told them the truth. Lee wanted to be different.

Flora's eyes widened. "Grandpa Winston?"

"Yeah. He started giving away his things. Just small stuff, nothing obvious. But I noticed. I told Grammy Charlotte, and she told me to mind my own business."

"What happened?"

Lee stared into her empty mug. "I was right."

Flora nodded. "That's the worst part. Being right."

They sat in silence for a moment. "You know what I wish someone had told me at your age?" said Lee.

"What?"

"You should trust yourself."

Flora glanced up, studying Lee's face for signs of insincerity. Finding none, she said, "Do you?"

"Do I what?"

"Trust yourself?"

"Well," said Lee, "I guess if I'm being honest . . . no."

Flora looked at Lee, her stare so piercing that Lee felt uncomfortable.

"I don't trust myself," Lee continued. "I guess I stopped hearing my true heart a long time ago. Now, when I try to hear it"— she shook her head—"I can't."

Flora's eyes did not move from Lee's and she said something so softly Lee couldn't hear her. Lee moved close and said, "What?"

"I have it too," murmured Flora, into Lee's hair.

Lee's blood went cold. "Flora," she said, "what are you saying?"

"Maybe everyone would be better off without me," whispered Flora, pressing her palms to her eyes and starting to shiver.

"Oh, sweetie," said Lee. Her gut seared with the horrible realization that Flora had the same anguish as she. "That's not true," she said. "Flora, that's not true. That voice—telling you lies— that's Depression, Flora. I hear it. I hear it too, little one. But it's not true. We need you. We need you."

"Is it like this for you?" said Flora.

"Yes."

"I hate the voice," said Flora.

"Flora," Lee said, "why have we been distant? I always felt like you didn't want me around."

Flora twisted her hands. "Grammy Charlotte and Mom . . . they always said you were fragile. You were going through a lot and we shouldn't bother you. . . ." She looked up at Lee. "I . . . handle everything myself. But inside . . ."

"Yeah," said Lee. "I know."

"And I was scared that if I told anyone about the voice in my head, they'd say I was fragile, too. That I'd become someone people had to protect . . . not someone who could help them."

"Oh, Flora. Being scared doesn't make you fragile. It makes you real." Lee held tight to her niece. "Listen," she said, "you need to promise me you'll tell your school nurse right away. Promise me, OK?"

"OK," said Flora softly. She pulled back from Lee, but her gaze stayed fixed—searching, hoping, as if Lee might offer something to keep her above the surface.

"Flora, there are medicines that can make the voice go away."

"Really?"

Lee wanted to tell her the truth, which was no, not really. Not forever.

She equivocated, "Your nurse can help you, Flora."

There was a sound from Flora's laptop. Flora leaned in to read.

"What is it?" asked Lee.

"Maya just found something."

"Flora—" said Lee, not wanting to change the subject.

"Mom's phone was ported out the day she left Athens. Maya just sent me the address where Mom's phone last connected before it was switched."

Lee stared at Flora, overwhelmed. "You have the address where your mom's phone connected on the day she left?"

"Yes."

"Write it down," said Lee. "And Flora?"

"Yes?"

"Thank you for trusting me."

56 REGAN WITHOUT FRANÇOIS

REGAN GRIPPED THE STEERING WHEEL OF HER RENTAL CAR, TEARS blurring her vision as she exited the Palazzo Casino & Spa. She turned and headed back toward Boğazköy Pass, pressing hard on the gas. How hopefully she had driven into this cheesy resort just days before! Now she felt dizzy and sick, visions of the ridiculously opulent lobby flashing in her mind—its weird mash-up of British colonial charm and Vegas glitz; the blinding light from gazillions of cascading crystal chandeliers; the massive grandfather clock mocking Regan as she waited and waited: alone, perspiring, wearing pink lululemon leggings.

Finally, Regan could no longer sit still on the low, ottoman-style couch. She checked into her room, thinking he would come to her in the night, wake her with kisses. Her hope withered on the second day, yet still she did not leave. How many days did she wait there for him? Her phone had stopped working; it just wouldn't connect. When at last she left the room, she was broken; forgot her wallet and passport in the safe.

Regan needed to turn around.

She needed to go home to her girls.

Were you supposed to accelerate into hairpin turns? Or decelerate? Regan wiped her eyes with the back of her hand and sped up as the mountain road twisted, revealing glimpses of the Mediterranean, the sunset making its waves gold. She flew past ancient olive groves, rocky gorges, and whitewashed villages perched on cliff sides. Regan blinked repeatedly, trying to clear her vision. She should stop, should pull over, should—

A wild animal burst from the scrubland.

Regan's mind went slow—*Was that a cat? A goat? Do goats come down from the mountains?*—and she jerked the wheel instinctively. The tires of her rental Renault lost their grip on the loose gravel. As her world tilted sideways, Regan saw them, her daughters. A vision of walking into her former home with newborn Flora, toddler Isabelle running to her, arms open, calling, *Mama!*

5⃞7⃞ LEE

ONCE LEE WAS IN HIS CAR, MARKOS VEERED INTO TRAFFIC. "TEN minutes to this address," he said. He was extremely calm, too calm—eerily calm, as if he knew devastation lay ahead.

"Flora says Regan's phone connected on the day she disappeared."

"And then no further activity. Yes, she sent the report. We don't know any more. It could have been disabled or she could be . . ."

"Inside the building," finished Lee.

"Correct."

"How long can someone survive . . ."

"I don't know."

They careened down a narrow street in a part of the city Lee had never visited. It seemed industrial; no cafés or pedestrians in sight. Lee's heart was a jackhammer. She saw the smoke first, then a building on fire. "Oh my God," she said. "Markos!"

"Γαμώ," muttered Markos. He pulled to the side of the road and checked his phone, his GPS. In silence, they watched jets of orange and yellow flame envelop a large structure.

"That's the warehouse?" said Lee.

"Yes."

"Where are the fire trucks?" cried Lee. "Where are the other police cars?" She opened her door, smelling smoke.

"Lee . . ." said Markos, holding her elbow.

She twisted away, her voice a wail of anguish, *"Why are we the only people here?"* Lee started to run toward the building. Windows shattered with sharp, distinct pops, and metal siding glowed a dull red as it warped. Thick columns of smoke rose, blackening the night sky.

"They're on the way!" said Markos. "They're on the way, Lee, stop!"

"Regan!" Lee yelled. "Regan!"

Regan had never recovered from the motel where Mr. Ragdale had taken her when she was fourteen years old. Regan had believed in her love story with her teacher completely. But facing the truth that he was a predator and she had been harmed—not loved—changed a fundamental part of Regan's psyche. Instead of becoming more vigilant about protecting herself, Regan seemed to think she was worthless and would take what she could get.

But she had divorced her abusive husband, the girls' father, Matt.

She had come all the way to Greece.

Lee would not allow her baby sister's story to end this way.

Waves of heat distorted the view, the air itself seeming to vibrate, the smoke acrid and thick. As she drew closer to the building, Lee started to choke. Her skin began to sear. For a moment, Lee stopped and put her hands on her knees, trying to inhale. When she bent over, she felt a blistering pain on the top of her head. Markos reached her and tried to bring her back.

Lee wrenched free. She stepped closer to the fire, then closer. If Regan was inside, she would die. Unless Lee got her out. There was no time to wait for whoever Markos said was coming. There was no time.

It was Lee or no one.

As always.

"Regan!" she cried.

Lee staggered forward but halted again. She couldn't breathe, and the pain of the fire on her body was monstrous. "I don't care if I die!" she screamed, saying the truth aloud for the first time. "I want to die!" she said, and she forced herself another pace closer and it was true, she wanted everything to end, she did, she wanted to die, but she stopped.

She couldn't do it. Something in her would not die.

Lee threw her head back and wailed.

She stepped away from the flames.

58 REGAN WITHOUT FRANÇOIS

REGAN HEARD VOICES. SHE TRIED TO MOVE AND COULD NOT. THE voices were not speaking Greek or English or any language she recognized. There was a light in her eyes. There was pressing on her hand, on her leg, and words she did not understand.

After the light, someone speaking English. "Do you know your name?" asked a man, a man in a doctor coat. She could not remember her name.

"Where am I?"

"İngilizce konuşuyor. What is your name?"

She shook her head. A deep blue space in her mind. Driving a car on a mountain road, but from where and toward what?

A nurse, a male nurse with a kind voice. "Here is a pen. You can draw and write down anything you remember about who you are."

Regan remembered the pay phone at her elementary school. Cool plastic in her hand. Her finger on cold metal. She remembered the pay phone at the bad place Mr. Ragdale had taken her. If she pressed the square buttons, she could go home. The number of her landline. If she had a quarter, she could call her mom. She did not know who or where she was, but she knew her home number by heart.

59 CORD

CORD FOUND A HALF BOTTLE OF HARVEYS BRISTOL CREAM, WHICH he drank from his grandmother's sherry glasses as he munched on Cheetos (when had Charlotte bought Cheetos?). He lay on a chaise longue and watched people play golf from Charlotte's patio. Did he care what they might think of him in his mother's pink bathrobe? He did not. He brought all of the old photo albums outside and paged through them, sipping daintily.

One of the newer albums was a testament to his own career. Charlotte, it seemed, had cut every clipping ever printed about Cord's VC firm. Snorting, he read an interview where he explained, "My father died of a sudden heart attack." After Winston's death, Cord told the interviewer, he'd learned to multitask to help his mom and siblings, and this attention to detail had served him well in the tech sector.

Lee and Charlotte had kept Winston's suicide a secret for decades! It was fucked-up and unhealthy, but also (honestly) impressive. The women in his family were fierce as hell, stubborn as mules. Charlotte had even cemented her fake narrative in a Walgreens photo album. Charlotte was a piece of work!

In the kitchen, Charlotte's wall phone rang. Cord knew it was creditors. He ignored it. Cord refilled a sherry glass and gazed at his mom's ancient magnolia trees. It was true that his nervous nature made him a good businessman. If you can't rest, you won't fuck up. Cord had made a work life where everyone and everything depended on him. Until this week!

His mind returned to the glow he'd felt earlier when he'd examined the pictures of Regan looking at him proudly. *I was such a good big brother,* he told himself sadly, drunkenly. Something about working through sherry in his grandmother's tiny crystal glasses made him especially maudlin.

The wall phone would not stop ringing! Cord heaved himself up from the chaise, went inside through the screen door, and picked up the receiver. "Hel-lo?" he said.

"Hello?"

"Regan?" Cord felt a shock of joy hearing his little sister's voice. "Regan!" he said.

"I need to come home now," said Regan, her voice a frightened monotone.

"What's going on, Reeg?"

"I'm done now and I need a ride home."

60 LEE

"LEE," SAID MARKOS, "YOUR SISTER HAS BEEN FOUND."

"Is she—"

"She is alive. Critical condition. She's been in a coma at Burhan Nalbantoğlu State Hospital. Your sister had no ID when hikers saw her car below the road between Kyrenia and Bellapais; the Turkish side of Cyprus. Turkish authorities don't cooperate directly with Greek police. She gained consciousness and called someone in your family who was able to identify her. They're arranging transport to Athens."

HOSPITAL REPORT
SOTIRIA GENERAL HOSPITAL

Department of Emergency Medicine / Τμήμα Επείγουσας Ιατρικής
PATIENT MEDICAL REPORT / ΙΑΤΡΙΚΗ ΕΚΘΕΣΗ ΑΣΘΕΝΟΥΣ
Patient name / Όνομα Ασθενούς: WILLINGHAM, Regan Marie
Age / Ηλικία: 42
Nationality / Εθνικότητα: American / Αμερικανίδα
ID / Passport / Διαβατήριο: USA 598447329
Method of arrival / Τρόπος Άφιξης: Helicopter medical evacuation /
Αεροδιακομιδή με Ελικόπτερο

PRESENTING CONDITION / ΚΑΤΑΣΤΑΣΗ ΠΡΟΣΕΛΕΥΣΗΣ:
Patient found by hikers inside vehicle at bottom of ravine off mountain
road between Kyrenia (Girne) and Bellapais village, near the Kyrenia
Mountain Range, Turkish-controlled Northern Cyprus. Vehicle discovered approximately 1.2 km east of Bellapais Abbey trailhead, below a
sharp downhill bend with no guardrail. Patient unconscious upon dis-
covery. Extraction performed by local emergency services with assistance from military patrol unit stationed at Kyrenia Pass checkpoint.

PHYSICAL EXAMINATION / ΦΥΣΙΚΗ ΕΞΕΤΑΣΗ:

Vital Signs / Ζωτικά Σημεία:

BP / ΑΠ: 82/54 mmHg (hypotensive / υποτασική)

Pulse / Σφυγμός: 128 bpm (tachycardic / ταχυκαρδία)

Temp / Θερμ: 35.2°C (hypothermic / υποθερμία)

O2 Sat / Κορεσμός: 91% on room air

Primary Findings / Κύρια Ευρήματα:

Severe dehydration / Σοβαρή Αφυδάτωση

Skin turgor severely decreased / Σημαντικά μειωμένη ελαστικότητα
    δέρματος

Mucous membranes dry / Ξηροί βλεννογόνοι

Estimated fluid deficit: 15–20% body weight / Εκτιμώμενο έλλειμμα
    υγρών: 15–20% σωματικού βάρους

Malnutrition / Υποσιτισμός

Weight: 48kg (reported normal weight 56kg)

Muscle wasting evident / Εμφανής μυϊκή ατροφία

Ketones present in urine / Παρουσία κετονών στα ούρα

Traumatic Injuries / Τραυματικές Κακώσεις

Laceration above right eye, 7cm, infected / Θλαστικό τραύμα πάνω
    από δεξιό μάτι, 7εκ, μολυσμένο

Right ankle fracture, displaced / Κάταγμα δεξιάς ποδοκνημικής, με
    μετατόπιση

Multiple contusions and abrasions / Πολλαπλές θλάσεις και εκδορές

Neurological / Νευρολογικά

Glasgow Coma Scale: 13/15 (E4, V4, M5)

Pupils reactive but sluggish / Κόρες αντιδραστικές αλλά βραδείες

Possible concussion / Πιθανή διάσειση

CT scan ordered / Αξονική τομογραφία διατάχθηκε

IDENTIFICATION / ΤΑΥΤΟΠΟΙΗΣΗ: Patient admitted without identification. Identification confirmed through dental records.

LABORATORY RESULTS / ΕΡΓΑΣΤΗΡΙΑΚΑ ΑΠΟΤΕΛΕΣΜΑΤΑ:

Sodium / Νάτριο: 152 mEq/L (H)

Potassium / Κάλιο: 2.8 mEq/L (L)

Creatinine / Κρεατινίνη: 2.1 mg/dL (H)

BUN / Ουρία: 68 mg/dL (H)

Glucose / Γλυκόζη: 52 mg/dL (L)

WBC / Λευκά: 16,000/μL (H)—suggesting infection/υποδηλώνει λοίμωξη

Hgb / Αιμοσφαιρίνη: 9.2 g/dL (L)

TREATMENT INITIATED / ΘΕΡΑΠΕΙΑ ΠΟΥ ΞΕΚΙΝΗΣΕ:

IV fluid resuscitation—0.9% NS 200ml/hr

Antibiotics: Ceftriaxone 2g IV

Wound debridement and suturing / Χειρουργικός καθαρισμός και συρραφή τραυμάτων

Right ankle immobilization pending orthopedic consultation / Ακινητοποίηση ποδοκνημικής

PSYCHOLOGICAL EVALUATION / ΨΥΧΟΛΟΓΙΚΗ ΕΚΤΙΜΗΣΗ:

Patient repeatedly asking for "François," believed to be romantic partner. States she was "meeting him at the hotel." No person by this name has presented at hospital. Patient becomes agitated when informed she has been missing for multiple days. Exhibits signs of emotional trauma. Psychiatric consultation requested.

Η ασθενής ζητά επανειλημμένα τον "François"—πιστεύεται ότι είναι ερωτικός σύντροφος. Δηλώνει ότι "συναντούσε τον στο ξενοδοχείο." Κανένα άτομο με αυτό το όνομα δεν έχει παρουσιαστεί στο νοσοκομείο. Η ασθενής γίνεται ανήσυχη όταν πληροφορείται ότι αγνοούνταν για ημέρες. Εμφανίζει σημεία συναισθηματικού τραύματος. Ζητήθηκε ψυχιατρική εκτίμηση.

PROGNOSIS / ΠΡΟΓΝΩΣΗ:

Guarded. Patient requires continued IV hydration, nutritional support, and wound care. Risk of acute kidney injury due to severe dehydration. Psychological support essential. Full recovery expected with appropriate treatment, though rehabilitation may be prolonged. Επιφυλακτική. Η ασθενής χρειάζεται συνεχή ενδοφλέβια ενυδάτωση, διατροφική υποστήριξη και φροντίδα τραυμάτων. Κίνδυνος οξείας νεφρικής βλάβης λόγω σοβαρής αφυδάτωσης. Η ψυχολογική υποστήριξη είναι απαραίτητη. Αναμένεται πλήρης ανάρρωση με κατάλληλη θεραπεία, αν και η αποκατάσταση μπορεί να είναι παρατεταμένη.

Attending Physician / Θεράπων Ιατρός: Dr. Evangelia Kostas / Δρ. Ευαγγελία Κώστας

License / Αριθμός Αδείας: 45789-GR

Signature / Υπογραφή: E. Kostas

62 LEE

say to her sister. There was no room for anger or recriminations. Lee would play *concerned*. She would act *loving*. She'd once portrayed a spurned wife on a police procedural and the director had told her to *exude love* when she reunited with the man playing her philandering ex who'd been beaten senseless on a New York street. (Might have been Long Island City.)

Would Regan be—as the actor playing her philandering ex-husband had been—struck with admiration? Would she be grateful? Would she cry and say, *Lee, I don't know what I would do without you!*

Hospital light had a way of making everyone look sick. Regan, sweet Regan, was conscious, propped against· pillows, her face gaunt beneath her bruises. A bandage wrapped her right ankle, and an IV dripped fluids into her arm. The doctors said she was lucky—dehydrated, malnourished—but alive. During her coma, she'd lost twenty pounds. She had been completely disoriented when she woke up, but the doctors said she now seemed to be functioning at full capacity.

Lee moved to the chair beside the bed. She'd rehearsed her role, and was ready to hide her fury and bewilderment and say,

You're alive, Regan. That's all that matters. . . . (She would pause here, lean toward her little sister, then whisper, *All that matters.*)

"Thank you for coming," said Regan, her voice weak. She pressed her hospital blanket between her fingers, pleating and un-pleating the thin fabric.

"Of course I came," Lee said, arranging her face into the ex-pression she'd practiced—concerned but capable, the sister who could handle anything. "You're alive, Regan," she began.

Regan's hands stilled on the blanket. "I hate myself," she said.

Lee leaned forward. "Your girls are incredible. Flora's been really strong. But they need their mom."

"I know what they need, Lee." Regan's voice was flat, and she wasn't meeting Lee's eyes.

"It was a lot," said Lee, wanting her sister to thank her, at least. "We were all just terrified. The police made me give a press conference—"

"Press conference?" Lee saw something sharp in Regan's ex-pression.

"We knew media attention would—"

"Media attention! Ohhhh, OK, I get it," said Regan, her voice venomous. Lee had not expected her sister to get venomous!

"I was trying to help," said Lee, venom inspiring venom (as always). "Everyone wanted—"

"Everyone wanted, or *you* wanted?" Regan sat up straighter in the bed, anger tightening her face.

"What is that supposed to mean?"

"It means you love pretending you're looking out for every-one else, but it always comes back to Lee Perkins in the spot-light." Regan's words were quiet but precise. "Tell me, Lee—how does it feel to be important again?"

"I was worried sick about you, Regan."

"I'm sure you were. But you were also enjoying it, right? Starring in your own missing-sister movie? All eyes on you?"

"That's not—you're not being fair, Reeg. I came here for you."

"No." Regan's words were exacting and mean as hell. "You came here because you were tired of feeling invisible."

"The girls—"

"The girls need their mother, not an aunt with a savior complex." Regan's voice grew in strength. "You think I don't know what this is? Even now, you're acting."

"I was trying to help!" Lee protested, but despite her affronted tone, she recognized the kernel of truth in her sister's accusations. Hadn't she felt more alive during the press conference than she had in months? Hadn't she been sickeningly thrilled when Markos called her to race to the warehouse?

"You were trying to matter." Regan leaned forward. "And it worked, didn't it? For a little while, you got to be the big sister holding everything together again."

Lee felt tears burning behind her eyes. "Regan, I love you."

"I know," said Regan, sinking back into her pillow. "I know. But you love being depended on, too. And honestly, Lee, I don't have the energy to make you feel important right now."

Lee stared at her sister. "What are you saying?"

"I'm saying, go home." Regan added, meanly, "Wherever that is for you."

"Regan . . ."

"I honestly do not have it in me to perform gratitude for you, big sister."

"But the girls—"

"The girls are fine. They have me. They have *their mother*."

"But you just—you just left them."

"Lee . . ." Regan paused, looking directly at her sister. "I maybe needed you a long time ago, but I don't need you any-more."

Lee felt the weight of all the years she should have protected Regan and didn't, all the ways she'd failed when it mattered. "I'm sorry I wasn't there for you when Mr. Ragdale—"

"Jesus." Regan's face went hard again. "It's a bit late for re-grets, OK? I want to talk to my daughters. Can you call my daugh-ters, please?"

"Of course," Lee managed.

Her hands shook as she dialed Flora's number.

"Mom? Is that you?"

"No," said Lee, "but she's right here. I'm at the hospital and—"

"Give me my mom!" Flora's voice cracked with longing—but not for Lee.

Never for Lee.

"Here's your mom," Lee said quietly, handing over the phone and turning to leave.

Regan's words echoed as Lee walked the long hallway to the hospital exit: *I don't need you anymore.*

Depression, patient as always, agreed: *No one needs you any-more. They would be better off with you gone.*

63 LEE

THE APARTMENT FELT SMALLER WHEN LEE RETURNED FROM THE hospital: the couch where she and the girls had cuddled together during the first nights waiting; the kitchen table where they'd scrutinized Regan's online activity and shared meals; assorted detritus of a teenager and young adult—shoes, hoodies, unmatched socks, hair ties, water bottles, charging cords. Lee felt as if she were standing among discarded props from a play, a show that had closed.

Flora smashed the apartment door open. "Auntie Lee! How's Mom?"

"She's good," said Lee robotically. "She'll be home soon."

Flora set her backpack down, her face hopeful and anxious. "Really? When?"

"Tomorrow or the next day, I think." Lee smiled brightly, trying to project hope.

"That's amazing," Flora said, bouncing on her heels. "Mom's OK! I can't believe it, Auntie Lee. I'm going to make dinner! That lentil soup from *Bon Appétit*? Grammy will be very excited."

Lee watched Flora. Sixteen years old and already carrying the weight of cooking, keeping the household running, trying so hard to be perfect and helpful that it made Lee want to shake her, grip her shoulders and say *something,* give Flora a shining pearl of wisdom that would free her from the lonely life she was assembling for herself: a life of never knowing who she actually was and what she, Flora, even wanted. The silencing of her heart, replacing her own desires with an overdeveloped ability to win others' approval. Lee wanted to cry, *Don't be like me!*

But her job here was done.

"Yum, lentil soup," said Lee.

REGAN HAD TOLD THE GIRLS SHE WASN'T ALLOWED ANY MORE VISI-
tors. Lee wasn't sure if her sister was lying, but Flora seemed to
buy it. Lee kept uneasily mum. That evening, after Flora's lentil
soup (which *was* delicious), Lee, Charlotte, and Flora went for ice
cream in the neighborhood.

(Lee texted Isabelle to ask if she was OK, and Isabelle sent a
text back saying, yessir im good. Isabelle was of age: Lee gave
the text a thumbs-up emoji but internally gave Isabelle a shrug
emoji.)

The ice cream café was tucked between a pharmacy and a
store crammed with tchotchkes, its front window displaying evil-
eye pendants. "What is the deal with the evil eye?" said Lee, looking at the rows of blue glass charms that seemed to stare back
from every surface—clipped to key chains, embedded in silver
jewelry, painted on ceramic tiles, and even adorning the handle of
a coffee cup.

"It's totally real," said Flora, lifting her slim wrist and showing
a beaded evil-eye bracelet. "Nico explained it to me—the eye pro-
tects you from jealousy and bad intentions—like if someone
gives you a nasty look or wishes you harm, the evil eye deflects it.
Even Nico's parents, who are professors, they still have them

hanging all over their house. Nico was serious about it when he gave me this one. He said I needed protection walking around Athens as a foreigner."

"A charm bracelet to ward off bad luck?" sniffed Charlotte. "That's ridiculous."

"I need one," said Lee, thinking of all the internet trolls and jealous actors who wished her harm . . . and also of Regan's fury.

"Well, I'm not going to *not* ward off bad luck," agreed Charlotte, and they went into the store and bought bracelets that matched Flora's.

At Da Vinci Gelato, Lee ordered her new favorite flavor, Kaimaki, which was creamy and slightly chewy with a pine-like herbal flavor. She added cherry syrup on top. "I should learn to make my own ice cream," she mused.

"You should," Charlotte agreed, tucking into a chocolate scoop. "But you won't."

"Mom's never been here," said Flora. "Let's bring her as soon as she comes home!" The trio fell silent—this was the first time any of them had said "when" with such certainty, and not "if."

"She's going to love this place," said Lee.

"Is her favorite flavor still pistachio?" asked Charlotte.

"Yes," said Flora.

"She always got pistachio! Even as a little girl," said Charlotte. "Such a sophisticated palate."

Lee smiled at her mom, who added, "Lee, you always wanted Oreo."

Lee, certain she'd just been insulted but not clear on the details, asked, "Wait, what's wrong with Oreo?"

Charlotte shrugged, making a moue with her bright lips. "A bit pedestrian," she noted.

Lee exhaled hard through her nose and did not respond.

On the walk back to Regan's apartment, they chatted about

Charlotte's new favorite Greek game show, *Rouk Zouk;* Flora's up-coming school trip to Nafplion, a walled city in the Peloponnese; and Isabelle and Anastasia, who were, according to Isabelle's Insta-gram, eating sushi at a nightclub on a beach (*im good* indeed, thought Lee). When the three women arrived at Regan's apart-ment, Lee could see Yassus hiding in his cozy spot behind an ole-ander shrub, waiting for Lee to be alone before he approached. As Charlotte rummaged through her oversize rattan purse from the J.Crew Factory outlet store (it was really more like a picnic basket than a purse), Flora blurted, "I'm just so happy! Mom's OK and it's like . . . it's like we're a family!"

"We are a family," said Lee.

"I suppose I'm the elderly matriarch," said Charlotte.

"The glamorous queen," said Lee.

Charlotte raised her eyebrows, considering, then nodded.

65 FLORA

FLORA HAD IMAGINED THE MOMENT FOR WEEKS: HER MOTHER COM-
ing home and pulling Flora into one of her overly long hugs,
whispering, "I'm sorry, baby, I'm sorry." They would make
PopBuster microwave popcorn, cue up the next "ep" of the show
they called "GG" (*Gilmore Girls*). Grammy Charlotte and Aunt
Lee could pack up and leave, or stay, whatever. Regan would
tell Flora everything, confess her lies, cry about the fact that
François was some criminal (or criminal syndicate) who only
wanted her money. Flora would console her mom, insist that
her mom deserved better and would find it, and Flora and
Regan would be closer than ever—just like Rory and Lorelai,
albeit in grimy Athens and not the fictional haven of Stars
Hollow.

But when her mom finally returned, she didn't rush into Flora's arms. Regan paused uncomfortably in the apartment doorway, looking smaller and bonier than Flora remembered, her face
an awful gray. Her mom's eyes scanned the apartment like she
was looking for something—or like she was planning her next
escape.

"Mom?" Flora had been sitting at the kitchen table with her

laptop, pretending to work on her computer science assignment but really just waiting. "Mom, you're home!" Flora said, trying to sound celebratory. Already a cold knowledge was growing in her gut.

"Sweetie," said Regan. She smiled, but it was fake and without apology, as if she was super worn-out from a long day—not as if she'd abandoned her children, given away all their money, and languished unconscious in a rural Turkish hospital, almost dying and leaving Flora alone in the world.

Flora closed her laptop and stood. Should she hug her mother? Wait for her mother to hug her? Her mom just stood there. "Are you OK?" she asked. "Do you hurt anywhere, Mom?"

"I'm fine, honey."

No, thought Flora, *no!* This couldn't be happening. Her mom wanted to return to the world of lies, to pretend everything was fine, and Flora couldn't do it. She could not do it. Auntie Lee had given her a taste of what life could be like if she said what was true, no matter how crummy the truth was, and Flora recoiled at the thought of returning to Faketown. It took *too much* from her to live in Faketown. It crushed your soul!

Every nerve ending on Flora's body hurt as she summoned the strength to confront Regan. "Mom," she said. She spoke loudly, in an intense almost-wail: "Mom! You're not fine, Mom!"

In her pocket, Regan's cell buzzed.

"Mom," said Flora. "Please, Mom . . ."

But Regan pulled out her new iPhone. Flora understood her expression. It was the look her mom got when she was deep in one of her François conversations, like the rest of the world had faded away.

"Mom!"

Regan held up a finger—just one second—and sadness grew

in Flora's chest and throat, pushing through her face and to her temples.

Regan turned from her daughter. Flora's jaw went loose with despair as she watched her mother choose the fantasy of being loved . . . over actually loving Flora, who was standing right there.

 ISABELLE

Anastasia's infinity pool, but she had to share the glamorous sight of a crystal champagne flute in her manicured hand, Anastasia's Cartier bracelet catching the late-afternoon sun. Not an hour later, her baby sister, Flora the narc, was standing at the marble entrance of the Boosalis home.

"Seriously?" said Flora as she was led outside by one of the staff, looking ridiculous in her school unform on such a hot afternoon by a pool. "This is where you've been?" said Flora.

"Do you blame me?"

"Isabelle, Mom's home and you haven't even seen her."

"Oh, does Mom care about me now? And not just François?"

Flora balled her fists, but she couldn't bring herself to lie. Just as Isabelle had suspected: Their mom had gone back to her romance scammer. Isabelle snorted and returned to editing selfies she'd taken, scrutinizing her own body. Her DMs were full of responses from other creators, photographers, and "talent scouts" wanting to work with her.

"Does anyone even wonder where I am?" said Isabelle. "Besides you, obviously?"

Flora bit her lip. Her cheeks were flushed—Isabelle's sister had probably run all the way here from the metro station. "Mom's been through a lot," Flora said weakly.

"We've all been through a lot." Isabelle uploaded a photo to her Instagram story. The responses started rolling in—fire emojis, heart-eyes, comments in multiple languages from accounts with impressive follower counts. One message caught her eye: Beautiful work. Are you interested in a professional opportunity? Isabelle had watched Aunt Lee command rooms by lifting her chin, had seen how men stumbled over themselves to help her, how women envied and copied her. Beauty was power—Lee had proven that. And if Lee could parlay her looks into fame and fortune, why couldn't Isabelle?

"What are you even doing here, Isabelle? Where's Anastasia?" Flora's voice had that edge it got when she was trying not to panic.

"I'm living my life, and Anastasia is asleep." Isabelle stretched out on the pool chaise. "Some of us don't want to spend our entire existence waiting for Mommy to remember we exist."

"You can't just never come home."

"Watch me." Isabelle held up her phone, reading another message: We should meet. I teach photography at several international schools. You are stunning. She felt a thrill—finally, people were acknowledging her talent. "Anastasia's parents are in Dubai for a month. At least."

"Your photos scare me, Iz," said Flora. "The ones from last night . . . you look—"

"Did you want to say *amazing*?" The photos from the underground party in Psyrri were mysterious and edgy, the kind of content that separated influencers from wannabes. "Photographers want to work with me, Flora."

"You look like a skeleton. Like a druggie, Isabelle."

"Maybe I'm trying to disappear." Isabelle felt something acidic and mean rising in her chest, the same feeling she got when she hadn't eaten all day and everything seemed too real and bright.

"Come home," Flora said quietly. "Please. I can't—I can't do this alone anymore."

There it was—a desperation Isabelle recognized.

"You want me to pretend we're a family?" Isabelle laughed, but it came out bitter. "Flora, grow up. Auntie Lee and Grammy Charlotte are leaving any day. We don't even have a mother."

"Don't say that."

"Why not? It's true." Isabelle watched Flora's face crumple slightly, saw the exact moment her sister decided to try harder, to be more perfect. It was pathetic . . . and exactly what Isabelle had done until she'd gotten smart.

"She needs us." Flora was close to tears. "And you need—we need each other."

"No," said Isabelle, standing up and pacing to the edge of the pool. "I'm eighteen, Flora. I have opportunities. Anastasia believes in me—unlike everybody else."

"I believe in you!"

"Appreciate, but you're a kid."

"What kind of opportunities?" Flora's voice was small, hungry. She wanted to be chosen too, Isabelle realized.

"The kind that get me the fuck out of here," said Isabelle.

"But what about me?"

"I'm sorry, Flor," said Isabelle, feeling a stab of guilt. Her sister was very alone. Someone would take advantage of her. But that wasn't Isabelle's responsibility—was it? "I'm going to New York. I can't let anything stop me."

"Not even me?" said Flora.

"Not even you," said Isabelle.

67 REGAN & FRANÇOIS

THE NOTIFICATIONS HAD BEEN PINGING FOR TWENTY MINUTES BE-
fore Regan finally woke, immediately grabbing her phone. François was upset—no, more than upset. Apoplectic. His messages
came in rapid succession, each one more urgent than the last:

> My darling, the lawyers need another
> payment today or they will freeze my
> accounts completely

> Please, my love, just €2,000 more and
> then we can be together forever

> Reqan, are you there? I am frightened.
> These people are dangerous

Regan's hands shook as she read. She'd already sent him
everything—her savings, the emergency fund, every cent Matt
had sent for child support. Her bank accounts were empty, her
credit cards maxed out. But François needed her. Who would
Regan even be, without him?

She'd never even asked about the Cyprus trip. As soon as her new phone started working, she got a beautiful note from François, who still loved her. And she couldn't stop responding, though she hated herself, she hated herself.

Regan stood in the hallway, caught between the sound of her daughter making dinner in the kitchen and François's messages on her screen. She thought of Flora's piggy bank—a ceramic elephant they'd painted together at the Oglethorpe Mall in Savannah. Flora had been saving for a computer of her own for months, carefully adding her allowance and birthday money to the childish elephant-shaped bank.

The girls' room was cluttered, too small for teenagers. Regan saw a high-heeled shoe overturned next to Isabelle's bed. Library books stacked neatly next to a reading lamp. A pair of beaded earrings, a tarot card ("The Tower"), a half-empty glass of juice. The elephant sat on the dresser, heavy with coins and carefully folded bills.

If she said no to François, he would vanish, and Regan would have to admit that she had ruined her life. She clung to the story that she and this man were building a future, even as a part of her knew that he had tricked her and disabled her phone while she was in a Turkish ravine . . . a part of her knew (of course she knew) he was a mirage.

She unscrewed the rubber stopper on the elephant's belly.

"Mom?"

Regan spun around, the bank still in her hands, bills scattered on Flora's dresser. Her daughter stood in the doorway, her expression confused, then stunned, then steely.

"You're stealing from me," said Flora, flatly.

"Don't be so dramatic. I'll pay you back," Regan said quickly, stuffing the bills into her pocket.

"Mom, I showed you all my research and interviews with romance scammers! I know how hard it is to break things off, but this person isn't real, Mom! You see that, Mom, right? I'm the only one you have left. And you're stealing from me."

"It's not stealing, Flora. I'm your mother."

"Oh, Mom," said Flora. Regan saw that Flora's empathy was turning to disgust. Regan's phone buzzed. She looked down automatically. "Go ahead, Mom," Flora said quietly. "Go ahead and answer your invisible boyfriend while you're holding my money."

Regan's thumb hovered over the phone. François was waiting. He needed her. He loved her. If he was fake, all that remained of Regan was shame.

The phone buzzed again: Time is running out

"I have to help him . . ." Regan clutched Flora's ceramic elephant bank.

"This is love?" Flora asked.

Regan looked at her baby daughter, saw a precious light in her eyes go dark.

She fled to the bathroom and locked the door behind her. Her hands shook as she counted Flora's money—€180. She sent François a message:

I found some more money. Heading to bank now, will send €180.

His response came immediately: You are an angel, my darling. But I need €1,800 more by tomorrow or everything is lost.

Regan stared at her reflection in the bathroom mirror. Who had she become?

She thought of all François's messages calling her "gorgeous," "stunning," "beautiful beyond words." For months, she'd been desired. Lee had always been the beautiful one, the one who got noticed. But François made Regan feel like she was the star of her own life, not a supporting character in Lee's.

François's next message came in: I love you more than life itself. You are saving me.

68 LEE

LEE'S DEPRESSION DID NOT ABATE. EVEN WHEN SHE SIGNED THE paperwork to play Lady Caroline in *Mad, Bad, and Dangerous to Know,* even as the media went insane, and Charlotte began to pack her things, and Isabelle posted disturbing photos on Instagram. Even as Lee fed Yassus every morning, and Val sent photos of fabulous rental apartments in Los Angeles, and every night Lee went outside and breathed in muggy Greek air, and Yassus lifted his big head and fixed her in his gaze. She filled his bowl and he came to her, the only creature honest about his hunger.

Regan's narrow street was quiet except for the evening sounds of Athens coming alive—plates clattering in kitchens, the hiss of meat hitting hot grills, voices calling from balcony to balcony. Ancient stones held the day's heat. Yet even in this hidden corner of Plaka, darkness found Lee.

Flora cleaned. Every surface gleamed, but Flora continued to putter around with her sponge and cleaning spray, a deranged domestic servant.

"Have you ever seen *The Jetsons*?" said Lee, rubbing her tired eyes. "It's an old cartoon. You're reminding me of Rosie, their robot maid."

"Is that a compliment, Auntie Lee?"

"No, honey. For the love of God, sit down."

Flora paused, still holding Questo cleaning fluid. "I just . . . I want everything to be . . ."

"Flora, seriously. Stop."

"I'm almost done."

"No, you're not!" Lee went into the kitchen and wrenched the bottle away. "You'll never be done! I know because I did this and it didn't work."

"Did what?" Flora glared at Lee, her hands clenching and un-clenching.

"I see myself in you, Flora," said Lee. "I've been through this. Please listen to me."

"Whatever," said Flora, moving to the living room, fluffing pillows that didn't need fluffing, straightening books that were already straight. She picked up Grammy Charlotte's reading glasses and polished them carefully before setting them back on the side table. Flora didn't speak, but her gestures cried out: *Please, won't anyone notice me?*

Lee remembered trying to hold their family together after her father's suicide. The same performance of usefulness, the same exhausting show. How could Lee warn Flora about a trap she was still inside? Lee herself had flown across an ocean to be needed. Watching Flora was like watching herself drown in slow motion.

Flora picked up Lee's purse off the coffee table and handed it to Lee.

"Flora, sweetheart, please just stop."

"You stop!" yelled Flora, whirling around. "No one is asking for your help or your opinions, Aunt Lee. Go back to Hollywood—Jesus!"

Lee inhaled.

She got it.

I told you, said Depression.

In a way, Lee was glad. There was nothing she could do to change Flora's path: Some patterns were just too strong to break.

69 CORD

landline, and Charlotte had informed Cord she wasn't returning to Wiley Bottom Road for some time. When the mayhem of Regan's rescue and homecoming subsided, Cord was left with himself, stuck in the rut he had created. He could relate to his sister's wild attempts to escape her reality. Cord had ridden his boozy wave of relapse right into dry land. What the hell was he going to do now?

He could go back to New York and continue being a workaholic, funding dopamine-pumping, brain-rewiring products. But Cord had to acknowledge that he was a wreck, freely using booze to avoid his misery. Was it profitable? Oh, yes. Was it sustainable? Maybe. But Cord was worn down. Adding to his mushed-to-a-nub feeling was a wild, uncomfortable hope that there was something more for him—a surprise ending, a plot twist.

He could go back to rehab. Cord had worked the Twelve Steps and he could work 'em again. He could call Handy or find a new sponsor. This would get him out of immediate danger.

Cord knew he should choose rehab over Manhattan. He went into Charlotte's kitchen where—he guessed correctly—she had a big, fat phone book. Cord licked his thumb and turned to "R."

His local rehabilitation options were slim: Men's Rez, Health Qwest, and Front Porch for Men, which sounded sexy but was assuredly not.

Cord put his head in his hands. *Uuuuugh:* the thought of intake, of a sterile room, of the twinge in his back that came when he sat in a metal chair. He didn't want to hear about other alcoholics' childhood traumas! *Fuuuck.*

The landline rang. "Yello?" he answered, slurping a microwaved mug of soup.

"Cord?"

"Regan," he said. "Hey. You're home?"

"I'm out of the hospital, yeah," said Regan.

"How are you feeling?"

"I can't stop," whispered Regan.

"What?" said Cord.

"I can't stop messaging him."

Cord closed his eyes. "You mean the guy?" he said. "The guy on the internet?"

"Yeah."

"OK," said Cord. "I get it, Reeg. I can't . . ."

"What?"

"I can't stop drinking," said Cord.

"Oh no," said Regan.

"Yeah," said Cord.

"Wait, Cord—why are you at Mom's house?"

Cord paused. "I have no idea."

Regan started to laugh. "We are a fucking mess," she said.

"No, we're not," said Cord, reflexively. He added, "I saw Oprah being interviewed on TV. She wrote a book and she said something really smart. Something about, don't ask what's wrong with you, ask *what's happened to you.*"

"Hmmm," said Regan. "Deep."

"No, but seriously." Cord sat in Charlotte's wood-and-rattan dining chair, the last of a set, and rested his elbow on Charlotte's little white desk, which had a great view of her bird feeder and the golf course. "I found your diaries in the bonus room," said Cord. "Or scrapbooks, whatever you call them."

"Collage," said Regan, with a hint of pride.

Cord opened an album, looked at a photo montage of his own young face. Regan had created a circle of Cord pictures around a photo of herself, sleeping.

"François tells me I can be an artist," said Regan. "He always texts back. I don't feel alone. And he's educated. He knows about art, helps me see what I'm doing. Without him . . . there isn't anyone. Who sees me."

"You said the same thing about Mr. Fucking Ragdale, your pedophile art teacher," said Cord.

"What?"

"I remember. We were in front of Savannah Country Day, waiting for Mom to pick us up. Mr. Fucking Ragdale pulls up in his Ford Pinto—a Ford Pinto, Regan! And I said, 'Don't get in his car,' and you said, 'I have to,' and I said, 'Don't do it,' and you said . . ."

"What? What did I say?"

Cord lowered his voice as if he were telling a dirty secret. "You said that if it weren't for Mr. Ragdale, there wouldn't be anyone. That without him, you would be invisible."

"Oh," said Regan. "I don't remember that."

"And you left. You got in the Pinto, Reeg. And you were wrong, because I was right there and *I* saw you!" Cord looked at an empty bottle of Barefoot Chardonnay he'd left on the little white desk. He yearned for the way two to three glasses of wine blurred everything, made life bearable, silenced his essential loneliness. "I was right there," he repeated.

"I—"

"But me seeing you didn't matter. How do you think that made me feel?"

"And I bet Mom was late. To pick you up."

"That she was."

"I love you, brother."

"I know."

Cord turned the page of Regan's scrapbook. He saw a drawing of a container of Elmer's glue, but in the place of the label, Regan had pasted Cord's graduation photo. Cord shook his head. He had once been the family coagulant. "Listen, Reeg," he said. "Let's be each other's sponsor. When I want to drink, I'll call you. When you want to text this guy, call me."

Regan was silent. "And you'll answer?"

"I'll take Mom's Jetta to the AT&T store in town right now," said Cord. "I'll get a new phone, and you'll be the first person I call."

"I'll answer, too," said Regan. "Even at three A.M. Whenever."

"Thanks," said Cord.

"I see you," said Regan. Cord nodded and wordlessly hung up the phone. He surprised himself by starting to cry.

The first day, he texted Regan almost constantly. But he didn't drink. They gave each other ridiculous challenges: At Jalapeños in Skidaway, order the most expensive item on the menu (Ultra Molcajete with steak, chicken, shrimp, and nopales; a delicious splurge at $26) and Go buy the grossest Greek snack and send a pic (oregano chips with banana cola).

For twenty-four hours, they were OK.

7 0 REGAN

THE FIRST THING REGAN THOUGHT ABOUT WHEN SHE OPENED HER eyes in the morning was François. Was he *really* a scammer, or was there a possibility that somehow . . . she was loved . . . that everything she *understood* was an elaborate fraud was . . . in some universe . . . real? His lavish attention had felt good. She wanted him to be real. Every minute she kept François blocked was like a sad, lonely year.

She missed him, and it hurt. There was no joy to take the place of François, only crushing shame, endless days to make it through, and worry.

At least her brother understood. She texted Cord: don't want to get out of bed.

He responded immediately: So don't

Regan grinned. She heard her girls getting ready for school but the thought of joining them was too hard. Without François, no one wished her *Good morning*. No one said, *You are beautiful*. Her daughters hated her, and with good reason. Cord texted again: Why can't I be normal? Why can't I just have a martini like a normal person?

Because you're a very special alcoholic, Regan wrote.

Lucky me, wrote Cord.

What time is it there?

3AM

Why are you awake?

Because I'm crazy.

Lee is leaving soon.

Have you talked to her?

Not really. Haha I think
she wishes I were gone
and she could steal the
girls.

Yikes.

Thanks for not judging.

I judge everyone constantly.

Me too.

So does Lee.

Yeah.

I'm closing my eyes.

Are you sober?

Yes.

I'm proud of you.

Are you going to text him?

No.

I'm proud of you, too.

7 1 CORD

OH, FOR THE LOVE OF GOD, THE AA MEETING WAS LOCATED AT HIS mom's awful Catholic church. Cord stared at the building, feeling sick. He'd spent countless Sunday mornings trapped in the pews of St. James the Less, often feeling dizzy and hot—childhood disassociation? And what the hell was the "less" part of St. James the Less? Cord asked the AI chatbot on his spanking new iPhone, who explained that "the less" also meant "the younger." Hm! That was completely useless knowledge—thanks for nothing, artificial intelligence!

His new phone had also come with the Sweethearts app installed. ("It's cute," the AT&T salesperson had said, "like a shortie in your pocket.") As he forced himself to walk toward the eerie white church (he had the feeling he was in a horror film), Cord received a love note from his "sweetheart." Cord's sweetheart said, I'm thinking about you—are you thinking about me?

There had to be some way to take the Sweethearts app off his phone; talk about creepy. But then he *was* actually thinking about his fake wife, wasn't he? And mightn't it be much easier to have a partner who didn't have needs or demands? A shortie in your pocket whom you didn't have to worry about? Whom you couldn't hurt?

What is a shortie? Cord asked AI.

"Shortie" is a term that can have several meanings depending on the context:

1. A slang term of endearment or nickname for someone who is short in height
2. A slang term sometimes used to refer to a woman or girlfriend (particularly in hip-hop culture)
3. In finance, a "shortie" or "shorty" can refer to a short-term investment or a short position (betting that a stock will decrease in value)
4. A short film or video
5. A short story or piece of writing
6. A short drink (as opposed to a tall one)
7. Short shorts or short pants

The meaning typically depends on the context in which it's used. Is there a specific context you're interested in?

Cord gritted his teeth—why did an AI answer end with an invitation to chat more? (He knew, of course, that it was all about user engagement but that didn't make it any less annoying.) Cord went back to his car, unlocked the door, tossed his phone in the vehicle, locked it, and strode into the church of his youth. Cord had been sober for maybe ten hours since the last green sip of the last bottle in Charlotte's liquor cabinet (crème de menthe). He saw a sign with a triangle, the symbol for AA meetings, and an arrow. The thought crossed his mind that he could ask his AI chatbot what, exactly, the meaning of the triangle was, but then he realized he had no phone and honestly *who cared about this random information?*

He pushed through a swinging door, following the signs. The hallway smelled of industrial cleaner and instant coffee. Room

204 was empty except for a few couches and chairs and a folding table holding a coffee urn and store-bought sugar cookies. The Twelve Steps were framed on the wall. Cord did feel powerless. He did. That was Step One, "Feeling Powerless." He wanted his phone and a Scotch.

Cord hesitated in the doorway, wondering if he had the wrong day. Without his fucking device, he didn't know what time it was. He had long coveted an Omega Speedmaster Gemini IV watch. He could afford it. Why didn't Cord treat himself?

A middle-aged woman emerged from a side room, carrying a stack of pamphlets.

"You're here for the meeting?" she asked, sinking into a chair. She had a child's pink barrette in her hair.

Cord nodded. He took four strides, sat on a couch, and examined his Hoka sneakers. He jammed a throw pillow under his lower back. When he had gone to meetings regularly, he'd usually brought a notebook and pen, just to have somewhere to look while people spoke. Sometimes, he'd taken notes or drawn elaborate castles with turrets and drawbridges.

A few people entered the room. They all seemed to be teenagers. One boy caught Cord's eye—lanky, with headphones around his neck and an oversize sweater despite the warm weather. His defensive posture, the careful way he scanned the room, reminded Cord of himself.

The teens glanced at Cord curiously as they arranged themselves in the circle, some sprawling, others sitting ramrod straight. When the room was full—about fifteen kids ranging from what looked like thirteen to eighteen—the facilitator addressed the group. "Is anyone a newcomer to Alateen today?"

"Oh, no," said Cord. "I thought this was AA. I'm sorry."

The kids' heads swiveled to stare at him. "AA is in an hour," said the woman.

"You can stay," said the kid with the headphones. "If you want."

"I never went to Alateen," said Cord. "I should have, probably." Some of the kids laughed; Cord felt buoyed. "I'm a double winner," explained Cord—this was "recovery speak" for a child of an alcoholic who had become an alcoholic.

"Stay, it's cool," another teen murmured.

"Is everyone comfortable with that?" said the woman in charge.

The teens exchanged glances. Finally, a girl with purple hair shrugged. "Whatever. It's fine."

"You are one of us," said the kid with the headphones in a Darth Vader voice. There were nods of agreement. Cord felt happier than he'd felt in a while. "Thanks," he said. "I'm Cord. I'm an alcoholic. And my dad was an alcoholic."

"Hi, Cord," the group responded in unison.

The facilitator took her place in the circle. "For those who are new today, my name is Hannah. My father was an alcoholic for most of my childhood. He finally got sober when I was seventeen, but by then I'd developed a lot of habits to protect myself—hypervigilance, people-pleasing, taking responsibility for everyone's feelings." She paused. "I've been attending Al-Anon for twelve years now, and I've learned that I didn't cause my father's drinking, I couldn't control it, and I couldn't cure it. But I could heal myself."

She glanced around the circle. "Today, we'll each have three minutes to share whatever's on our minds. No one will interrupt or respond directly to what you say. This is a safe space to express yourself without judgment." Hannah placed a small timer on her chair arm. "Who would like to begin?"

The room was quiet for a moment. Then the purple-haired girl raised her hand.

"I'm Dani," she said. "My dad's been sober for almost a

year . . . this time." She stared at her hands. "He missed my band concert again last week. Not because he was drinking, but because he was at a meeting. I know I'm supposed to be supportive of his recovery, but sometimes it feels like nothing's really changed. He's still not around." She fell silent, and for over a full minute, no one spoke. The timer went off softly, and Dani nodded once, indicating she was finished.

A boy with glasses raised his hand.

"I'm Alex. My mom promises things are different now. She's got six months sober. But I still find myself checking the recycling bin for bottles. I still get nervous when she laughs too loud. I don't know how to stop waiting for the other shoe to drop." Alex looked around, then down at his lap. "That's all."

One by one, the teens shared their stories. No one responded, no one offered advice. Just three minutes of raw truth, followed by silence, then another voice. Cord sat quietly, absorbing their words, seeing himself in their hypervigilance, their premature responsibility, their exhaustion.

When it was the lanky boy's turn, he spoke so softly Cord had to lean forward.

"I'm Miguel. My dad went to rehab four months ago. Now he's home, and everyone acts like our problems are over. But he goes into the garage every night for hours. My mom makes excuses for him. And I'm the only one who helps my little sister with her homework."

Cord bit the inside of his lip. How many times had he checked Regan's math problems while their father was "working" and their mother was "resting"?

"The worst part is that it's like I *know* everything's going to fall apart again. I just want to be a normal kid."

The timer went off. Miguel nodded and leaned back in his chair. Hannah turned to Cord. "Would you like to share?"

Cord hadn't planned on saying anything, but he found himself nodding. "I'm Cord. I'm an alcoholic." He looked around the circle, at these kids whose experiences mirrored his own. "When I was your age, I was like many of you. I mean, my sisters and I took care of ourselves . . . we took care of each other. We stayed out of my father's way when he was in a mood, but I was always scanning for danger."

The timer ticked quietly.

"That need to take care of everyone, to control every situation—it followed me into adulthood. I built a career around fixing problems, controlling outcomes. I became very successful, but I never learned how to just . . . be."

Cord sighed, allowing himself to speak his truth. "And then I started drinking too. Even though I swore I never would. I used alcohol the same way my dad did—to just . . . shut it off, to stop feeling responsible for everyone else's happiness."

The kids were watching him intently now, without the skepticism they'd shown earlier.

"I'm uh, I've been sober for a day. Not even a day—like ten hours. Again. I've been here before. I'm still learning that I can't fix everything—can't fix my partner, can't fix my sister, can't fix myself through sheer force of will." He met Miguel's eyes briefly. "The patterns can be broken. They're hard as hell to break, but it's possible. I believe that. I do."

The timer sounded. Cord nodded, suddenly aware of how exposed he felt.

Hannah thanked everyone for sharing and concluded the meeting with the Serenity Prayer. They all stood in a circle, held hands, and said, "God, grant me the serenity to accept the things I cannot change, the courage to change the things I can, and the wisdom to know the difference."

The teens began to disperse. Cord hung back, not sure whether to wait for the AA meeting or just go back to Charlotte's. As he was gathering his things, the boy named Miguel approached him hesitantly. "Hey," Miguel said, his hands jammed in his pockets.

"Hey," Cord replied.

"I was wondering . . ." Miguel paused, clearly uncomfortable. "Um, I'm supposed to get a sponsor."

Cord blinked in surprise. "Oh, I can't be a sponsor, Miguel. I'm, like, at Step One."

Miguel shrugged one shoulder. "Yeah, got it. Sorry. I just . . . man, it's tough being a gay kid in this town. You wouldn't know." The kid seemed simultaneously defiant and terrified, as if expecting rejection but daring Cord to say something about his sexuality.

"Oh, Miguel, I *do* know," said Cord. They stood in silence for a moment. "Want to grab a coffee?" said Cord.

Miguel looked up, surprised. "Really?"

"Really."

A cautious smile spread across Miguel's face. "Yeah," he said. "Sure. That would be cool."

72 LEE

AS SHE KNEW IT EVENTUALLY WOULD, DEPRESSION BECAME TOO strong and painful for Lee to bear. Her sister's words—*You love pretending you're looking out for everyone else, but it always comes back to Lee Perkins in the spotlight*—echoed in her ears as she stuffed things in her suitcase.

In her mind's eye, Lee could imagine herself back in Los Angeles, swanning around the circuit, accepting accolades for her noble journey across the ocean to save her sister. She'd probably tear up a little when she told her tale, splay her fingers on her chest, inhabit the brave big sister who'd put her career on hold for family. The narrative was already crystallizing, another perfect anecdote for talk show appearances.

God, Regan was right about her. Had every moment of care, every rescue, every time she'd dropped everything to help—had it all been a charade? To quote Markos the cop, possible.

Possible, it was all—and always—a show.

Even her love felt suspect now. Did she love Flora and Isabelle, or did she love being the one they called when everything fell apart?

On her phone, Lee checked in for her flight from Athens to LAX. Flight 447 departed the next day at 2:15 P.M., an eleven-hour flight. Lee wouldn't make it to touchdown. She wasn't going back to a life of clinging to a dull version of sanity, Depression whispering in her ear day and night. Somewhere over the Atlantic, she could let go. The offer of a massive film role didn't bring her solace. She was not needed by anyone, all the calibrated meds weren't helping enough, and there was no reason to suffer any longer. It was too much, and that was OK. She'd made a journey to save her family, and now it was time to save herself.

Lee's boarding pass appeared on her screen. Seat 3A, first class.

Pure, clean relief flooded through her; it made her shoulders drop and her breathing slow. She had a plan. She had control. She didn't have to figure out how to live. Not anymore.

Everything she'd told herself about love, about family, about being the person others could count on—lies. Pretty lies she'd wrapped around an ugly desire to be necessary, a search for a way to escape the fact that she had nothing to offer, that she was empty and in pain.

One last performance to go.

73 REGAN

REGAN WAITED FOR HER GIRLS IN THE AMERICAN SCHOOL OF ATHENS pickup line. Although the other moms waved to her kindly, Regan was sure they thought she was a goddamn idiot. She *was* a goddamn idiot. It took all her strength to resist the desire to flee, to drive away and text François . . . allow herself the pleasure of hope and possibility. She bit her tongue and held one hand with the other and she sat still and watched the door of her daughters' beautiful school.

She texted Cord: I can't do it.

You can.

Do I have to?

Yes.

The night before, as they chatted, Cord told Regan that Step Nine, "Making Amends," would help ease her shame. "The shame makes you go back out," said Cord, using AA-speak. "Going back out" meant drinking for Cord . . . for Regan it was contacting François. It was incredible how similar their recoveries had turned out to be. "Just tell the girls you're sorry and you know it was a scam and it's over."

"You make it sound easy."

"Oh, no, it's the hardest thing you'll ever do. But you're

strong, Reeg. Look at all you've done already. You can do this."

A bell rang, and girls in uniforms poured into the front courtyard, some running to parents, others gathering into groups and standing on their own. When Regan saw Flora, she started the engine and rolled her window down. "I'm here! Flora!" she cried. Flora turned, looking surprised, nervous when she spotted her mom. Flora approached her sister, who was surrounded by a crowd, grabbed her hand, and spoke to her. Both girls came to Regan's car and got in the back seat.

"Why are you here?" said Isabelle, furiously. "We take the metro."

"I know, but I need to talk to you both."

The girls were silent. Regan drove the car down a side street and pulled over, parking. She looked at her hands as she said, "I was scammed. I get it now. I am . . . I am heartbroken about what I put you through. It was dumb and I hate myself, girls. I see it now, and it's over. It's over and I'm sorry. I know I can never . . . I know you will never trust me again. And I wish I could go back, but it is what it is and I messed up and I hurt you. My job is to love you and I—"

Regan stopped talking because her daughters had unbuckled their seatbelts and exited the car. Each slammed a door, leaving Regan utterly alone. She began to cry. They had abandoned her, and she deserved this. She put her palms to her face.

Regan's door and the passenger door opened, and Flora and Isabelle tumbled into their mother, embracing her from both sides. Regan kept crying. Flora started to cry. "We love you, Mom." Isabelle said, "Jesus, guys, enough with the waterworks!" Despite her mean tone, Isabelle held Regan the tightest.

Regan did not deserve forgiveness, but Flora and Isabelle gave it to her anyway.

74 CHARLOTTE

CHARLOTTE STOOD IN REGAN'S KITCHEN, WATCHING SMOKE RISE FROM a pan of scorched chicken bits. Greek appliances were the *worst*! There was the oven, which displayed temperature in Celsius and wasn't accurate or consistent anyway; the water heater that demanded you plan your shower thirty minutes in advance so it had time to warm up to tepid; the freestanding AC unit that was utterly incomprehensible with its tubes and buttons; and worst of all—the bane of Charlotte's existence—the stove. Turn the burner knob to Medium, and you might get a low simmer (*Hello, salmonella's on the menu!*) or flames leaping high into the air, incinerating your dinner and threatening to incinerate you.

Charlotte dumped the pan into Regan's sink. She'd found the recipe for "Mom's Famous Lemon Chicken" in Regan's recipe book, handwritten. It was Charlotte's handwriting, yet she had no memory of ever making lemon chicken, much less getting famous for it.

"Grammy, what happened?" Flora ran in with a dish towel, batting at the smoke.

"I just stepped away for a moment," Charlotte lied. She'd been in the living room, halfway through a glass of chardonnay, staring at her phone and willing it to ring with a call from Paros. (Or a call from *anyone*.)

She wanted a reason to leave this dilapidated apartment!

If Paros called, she could leave this dilapidated apartment!

Charlotte went into Regan's bathroom and stared at her face in the mirror, which Flora had recently Windexed. Her skin was no longer elastic, and her eyes seemed dull. Charlotte wanted more days, more love, more kisses . . . another adventure! To press her saggy cheek to a man's face, breathe him in. She wanted to grab a man's bottom in her palms. How could she be elderly when she was still filled with yearning?

"Grammy?" Flora knocked softly.

"Just a moment!" Charlotte called, voice artificially bright. She reapplied lipstick with a shaking hand. In the mirror, she practiced her smile.

"Are you OK?"

"I'm fine!" called Charlotte. And then, as if God himself had heard her prayers, her cellphone rang.

75 PAROS

ONCE A WEEK, PAROS WAS PULLED FROM HIS DUTIES IN THE SLOOP Shop to teach knot-tying to the guests at the Tropical Bar. His class came at the end of Eduardo's tutorial on creating bird sculptures from watermelon, and before Israel's "Rum Cocktail Master Class."

After his class, Monica cornered Paros and said, "I've got something for you, handsome." She winked (happily married for decades, Monica had done her damnedest to retain her flirtatious ways) and handed Paros a paper letter in a paper envelope, the first he had ever received on board. It was a miracle the letter had reached him at all; someone at home had crossed out "Mr. Paros Georgiou, Ikaria Island" and written "Panagiotis Georgiou, *The Flying Star,* Port of Piraeus"—his family had never liked the fact that he'd had to choose an "Americanized" name to work on cruise ships. But Paros loved his snappy nickname . . . after all, it was the name Charlotte cried out in her giant bed as they moved atop her heavenly "pillowtop" mattress. . . .

Oh, Paros! Paros, yes!

He recognized Charlotte's handwriting at once, the swoops and curlicues only an American would have the audacity to create. Charlotte—a beautiful peacock, a scared little chestnut. He had placed his heart in her bejeweled fingers. He took the letter below deck, ignoring Monica's nosy gaze and the implications of her wiggling eyebrows.

Paros shared his crew quarters with three other men. He wanted solitude to open what he desperately hoped was a love note, and climbed down the narrow ladder that led into the engine room, a dim chamber deep within the ship's hull. Grease-streaked pipes and steel were illuminated by bare, overhead bulbs, and the air was heavy with the scent of diesel fuel. As Paros carefully slid his thumb along the envelope's edge, easing it open, he felt the ship's engine vibrating through the floor beneath him.

Charlotte wrote that her daughter Regan was missing in Greece—shocking words that struck Paros like a blow. The thought of a child—even a grown one—lost in a foreign country overwhelmed him with helplessness and fear.

But then, Charlotte's tone changed. Tender endearments softened her harsh news. Charlotte wrote that she had made "terrible mistakes" and was coming to Greece. She offered, once her daughter was found safe, to visit his farm and kiss him. Paros closed his eyes and thanked God. The farm was now owned by his sons-in-law, but he knew the land held no worth for Charlotte.

The Flying Star sailing ship, however, she would adore, especially the Tropical Bar, which was stocked with chardonnay. She would admire the sixteen canvas sails unfurling like wings under towering masts.

When they had shopped together at an antique store in Savannah, in fact, she had admired a painting of two bulldogs in sailor costumes aboard a four-masted barquentine, and Paros had delighted his Charlotte by purchasing the artwork. He knew that she had hung the painting of bulldogs on a ship in her guest room, where her adult children slept when they came to visit.

Paros swooned. If Charlotte came aboard—maybe renting an

Owner's Cabin, why not?—Paros could join her at sunset. He could explain every detail of the complex rigging while Charlotte ignored him completely and knew herself to be the most fashionable and fabulous woman on deck. Charlotte belonged on this glorious vessel!

Paros folded the letter carefully. Charlotte's family was in crisis—and in her time of need, she was reaching for him. Charlotte had sent her cellular phone number. Paros went to Captain Pedro at once to request a guest aboard the ship. "An American?" said the captain, who was Argentine.

"Yes," said Paros.

"She is your lady friend?"

Paros's heart swelled with joy. "Yes," he said proudly, "her name is Charlotte."

76 CORD

CORD CONSIDERED FLYING TO GREECE. HE ALMOST RETURNED TO New York. But he was frozen, stuck in Savannah. *Do the next right thing,* they said in the rooms, yet another insipid and lifesaving AA platitude. He woke up, drank coffee, read the Big Book, went to meetings, slept in his mother's bed.

Hello, Step One, my old friend. I'm here to work through you again!

Cord stayed sober. At the Palmetto Shores gym, he lifted and did cardio. The only people he shared his new phone number with were Regan and Giovanni, who texted him to fuck off, which seemed fair. Giovanni added, Not trying to be mean, but I honestly need a break from this.

I love you and I understand completely, Cord responded.

He emailed NYC Ventures that he was on an extended mental health break, and Jacobey responded, "Take care, man," cc'ing HR. With the help of a Reddit hacker forum, he removed the Sweethearts app from his phone, then deleted Instagram, the *New York Times* app, Apple News, Facebook, Snapchat, Bluesky, and Twitter.

Cord met Miguel at Sandfly Coffee, paying for lattes and commiserating with the kid about growing up gay in suburban Savannah. As Cord had been at his age, Miguel was tough, capable, and worried he'd end up alone. He needed nothing from Cord but company.

The strangest development was Cord's text relationship with Regan. He should have been texting a sponsor when he wanted to drink, but instead he sent notes and emojis to his sister. He sent a fire emoji when he lingered at Publix, dangerously close to putting his hand on the elegant neck of a bottle of wine. She texted back a heart-hands emoji, and this helped him keep walking toward the bakery, where he bought a glazed donut or three. He sometimes ate one before he reached the register, but he "kept his side of the street clean," fessing up and paying the forty-five cents.

For her part, Regan would text Cord a broken-heart emoji when she wanted to contact her scam lover, François. Cord would text back heart-hands. Did it help her resist? Cord believed it did.

77 CHARLOTTE

CHARLOTTE TOOK A TAXI TO THE PORT OF PIRAEUS. PAROS HAD TOLD her during his thrilling phone call that she would find *The Flying Star* easily, as it was the only tall sailing ship docked alongside megaliners. "A sailing ship! How romantic," Charlotte purred.

"It was the job I was offered," said Paros. "And Charlotte? Please adjust your expectations. A tall sailing ship is not for everyone."

Charlotte did love her luxuries—her golf cart, a walk-in closet filled with clothes. And was this really the time for her to go chasing love? Yes, Regan had been located and brought back to her girls, but she was obviously struggling. Charlotte pushed the thought away. She herself was not getting any younger! As the disco song said, this was her *last chance for romance.*

Charlotte could see Donna Summer in her mind's eye, wearing a sequined pantsuit and imploring Charlotte to *dance the last dance tonight.* Charlotte nodded, her mind made up.

Her taxi descended from the heights of Athens toward Piraeus; the city revealing itself in layers—Byzantine churches nestled between apartment blocks, outdoor tavernas where old men played backgammon under grape arbors, balconies dripping with geraniums in recycled olive oil tins. The Mediterranean stretched before them, dotted with ferries heading to islands that promised escape, transformation, or both. Charlotte remembered her first journey to the port, before she had known what it felt like to explode in passion.

Now she knew. And somehow, she had let Paros go, along with his tender kisses and erotic maneuvers. Charlotte had become a doddering, albeit soigné, old woman. She forgot much of what happened to her or was said to her—famous lemon chicken? Remaining cheerful at age eighty-one was, she knew, a matter of calculated ignorance and strategic denial. But what was the alternative? Who the heck wanted to ponder the sadness of waking alone, the fear of falling over and breaking your paper chopstick bones?

Quelle horreur, but no one wanted to think about these indignities, least of all Charlotte.

Anyhoo, her cab stopped, bad brakes squealing, and Charlotte opened her compact to check her lipstick, mascara, and silver eye shadow. She'd used the nose hair trimmer her best friend, Minnie, now dead for a decade, had given her as a joke one year during her golf group's Secret Santa cocktail party. Minnie's joke gift had turned out to be useful when wiry hairs started growing past Charlotte's nostrils.

She wore white Capri pants, a navy-and-white-striped sweater, and gold, anchor-shaped earrings. (OK, *gold-plated,* but from the Ralph Lauren outlet store on Hilton Head Island.) This was the best she was going to look. It was time.

"Ευχαριστώ, γεια," said the driver.

"And the same to you!" said Charlotte.

But instead of bounding from the malodorous car, Charlotte remained still. The driver stared at her in his rearview mirror and raised his swarthy eyebrows. His pupils were the color of chocolate, his expression kind and a bit pitying. He probably thought she was a lonely heiress going on vacation by herself, not a single gal having a rendezvous with her Greek beau, the former love of her life, her partner in a torrid Mediterranean tryst on the high seas.

"Ευχαριστώ, γεια," he repeated.

"Yes, I heard you," said Charlotte.

"You need . . . assistance?" said the driver.

Feeling guilty, Charlotte pulled out her phone and called Lee, back at Regan's apartment. "Lee, darling? I'm about to board Paros's ship for—well, I don't know how long. But should I stay? Do they need me? Do you need me, Lee Lee?"

Lee's voice sounded tired but determined. "We're fine."

"I love you, Lee Lee. Call me if anything changes. I mean it."

After hanging up, Charlotte stared at her reflection in the taxi window. For decades, she'd been the family matriarch in name only. Lee had actually raised Regan and Cord after Winston died. Now her granddaughters needed stability, and she was running off with a man. But Charlotte didn't have long left! She wanted to be happy!

"Adios," said Charlotte, and of course she knew that "adios" wasn't Greek, but the Spanish farewell felt appropriately dramatic. "Adios, amigo!" she said, throwing open the taxi door. "Au revoir!" she added, for good measure.

She stepped into mayhem, joining a river of cruisers dragging giant wheeled suitcases toward megaliners, as she had once done herself. One man wore a T-shirt that said FEED ME BEER AND WATCH ME DANCE.

Charlotte shuddered.

She felt very alone. And yet, oh, the human heart, mused Charlotte: Despite the trials of life, the human heart yearned for love! Her human heart, anyway.

Across the parking lot, lit by bright sunlight, she saw her paramour. Paros, too, had aged, but he wore a trim white uniform with epaulets and dashing sunglasses. He looked important, gruff, and Marlon Brando–esque. Charlotte was proud that he had worked his way up, and was now manning the gift shop inside *The Flying Star*. In between colossal, gaudy (but fun, oh so fun) cruise ships, Paros's sailboat was breathtaking—its hull gleaming white, its many sails rippling in the wind.

Her hull—Paros had told Charlotte that you were supposed to call your ship "she."

She had gleaming mahogany rails, bright brass accents, a small gangway staffed by men in uniform. Staring at such a ship made Charlotte feel as if she were living in another time, boarding a vessel to sail across an ocean and start an unknown life.

Ah, if only she were beginning again.

Was it possible—could it be—that she was?

78 CORD

CORD WAS HALFWAY THROUGH HIS MORNING ROUTINE WHEN THE doorbell rang. He put down his mother's M.A. Hadley ceramic mug (the one with the little pig). *The New York Times* was open to the Arts section on the counter. Cord assumed that his mother would cancel the *Times* at some point, if she really were moving permanently into the Deluxe Cabin aboard *The Flying Star* tall sailing ship. Then again, Cord was the one who was paying for her Deluxe Cabin indefinitely, including an unlimited tab at the Tropical Bar . . . maybe she'd let him keep the newspaper.

Cord had also (happily) paid off Regan's debts, bought her apartment outright, and set up a monthly fund for her and the girls with two caveats: no renting rooms to random strangers and no Bitcoin (or otherwise suspicious) trading. He kept a close eye on her financial transactions and she, in turn, checked in to see that he was going to AA meetings . . . even calling Handy and giving him Cord's new phone number. Flora had offered to spy on Regan and Cord told her no way in hell—if Flora was going to go to Harvard, she had better things to be doing with her time than snooping on her mom.

So far, so good. Lee had even written Cord a long, sort of

maudlin e-mail about how much she loved him and believed in him. He wrote back that he loved her, too.

Charlotte's bell sounded again. Cord was honestly not in the mood for chitchat with one of his mom's friends—they popped by periodically, wondering why they hadn't seen her on the golf course or at Wine Down Wednesday. All of them were thrilled to encounter Cord—he'd racked up weeks of happy-hour invites.

The current caller was tenacious. The bell rang another few times, and finally Cord called, "Com-ing!"

He tightened his mother's bathrobe and opened the door.

It was Giovanni on the porch.

Gio carried his ratty old backpack—the one he'd hitchhiked with across Italy—and had dark circles under his eyes. His curls were shorter, and he wore a plain black T-shirt and jeans. "Hi," he said.

Cord was speechless and terrified.

Giovanni shifted his weight. "Can I come in?"

Cord stepped aside, watching as Giovanni took in the living room with its floral sofa, family photos, and large wicker alligator grimacing next to an end table. Giovanni paused at a framed photo of young Cord: skinny, wielding a baseball bat.

"This is where you come from," Giovanni said quietly.

"It's where I ran from," Cord clarified. "Coffee?"

Giovanni nodded, following him into the bright yellow kitchen. Cord poured a mug and slid it across the counter.

"How's Regan?" Giovanni asked, taking a sip.

"Better. She's home with the girls." Cord sat at the kitchen island. "Still struggling, but OK. We have a little text support network going, me and Reeg."

Giovanni took the seat across from him. "How are you?"

"Twenty-three days sober. Again."

"That's good, Cord."

"One of the many, many cheesy mottos of the program is 'Do

the next right thing,' " Cord said. "I'm trying. To do the next right thing."

The silence between them felt delicate. Cord found himself noticing details—the small scar above Giovanni's eyebrow, the dimple in his chin—all the familiar landmarks of a face he'd memorized. "Why are you here, Gio? I thought you needed a break from all this. From *me*."

Giovanni wrapped his hands around the mug. "You couldn't even say goodbye to my face."

"I'm sorry. You deserve better. We both know you deserve better."

"That's a cop-out."

"I'm trying, love. I'm trying again." A silence fell between them, broken only by the ticking of Charlotte's wall clock.

Giovanni was quiet for so long that Cord thought he might get up and leave. "I didn't fly to Savannah for closure," Giovanni said finally. "I could have had that in a phone call."

"Then why?"

"My therapist says when you love an addict, you don't get to plan ahead. You can take what you get for one day, day after day . . . or you can walk away."

"That's fucking bleak," said Cord. "But it's maybe true. I hate that. I hate that for us. I hate that for you."

"Yeah, but it's real, Cord. Who knows how long we have, any of us."

"Not exactly the fairy tale we talked about," said Cord. "White picket fence, joint Hamptons house, his-and-his monogrammed towels."

"Seize the day," said Giovanni. "That's what I want now. I want all the joy. I want all the joy, today, with you."

The happiness that rushed through Cord was so strong he stopped breathing. "Giovanni . . ." he managed.

Giovanni held up his hand. "I've got two weeks before rehearsals start and the theater kids take over my life," he said. "I thought I might spend them here. If that's OK."

Cord nodded, overcome.

"I want to go to the Pirates' House, and I want to see some real-life alligators, and I want to drive Charlotte's golf cart around the links."

"I can make all that happen for you," said Cord. "For us."

"Good," said Giovanni. "I packed all preppy outfits, Cord—Sperry Top-Siders, pants with whales, pink shorts . . ."

Cord moved close to his love.

". . . a pale blue Izod I thrifted, a Vineyard Vines tie, and a T-shirt that says PICKLEBALL FOR ALL."

Cord took Giovanni's face in his hands, but paused.

"You can kiss me," said Giovanni.

Cord held Giovanni's face, closed his eyes, kissed him tenderly. He inhaled the smell of coming home.

79 LEE

LEE CHECKED HER PHONE: ALMOST TEN—TIME TO FEED YASSUS ONCE
more and call a car to the airport. The timing felt appropriate—
she'd take care of the last creature who needed her, then go. In
her purse, Lee had twenty-eight pills wrapped in a silk scarf,
enough sedative-hypnotic to set her free.

She folded her pajamas, her movements slow and meditative.
The Plaka apartment was spookily silent. Charlotte had reunited
with Paros, packed up her monogrammed duffel, and boarded a
tall sailing ship. The girls were usually in their room or busy with
school friends and activities. Lee sipped yet another cup of instant coffee, ready to stop haunting a space where she no longer
belonged.

She knocked on the girls' bedroom door. "I'm heading out
soon."

"OK," came Isabelle's muffled voice through the wood.

"Bye," called Flora.

Lee pushed the door open. Both girls were on their beds, staring at devices—Flora cross-legged with her laptop open beside
her, probably doing homework even though it was Saturday, Isabelle sprawled across her comforter, scrolling. The girls glanced

up briefly, their faces blank. Lee remembered how they had clung to her when she first arrived.

Looking at them, Lee realized she wasn't even seeing Flora and Isabelle—she was seeing problems she'd failed to solve. Flora's compulsive studying, Isabelle's practiced indifference. Even now, she was cataloging their damage instead of simply . . . loving them.

"I'll call when I land," Lee said, though she knew she wouldn't. There would be no landing, no calls, no checking in. Just allowing herself to sleep in one of those wonderful first-class cubicles, blocked from prying eyes. Lee would eat the warm nuts before takeoff, a hot fudge sundae in the dark, then press the button that would extend her seat into a cozy, completely flat nest. The pills, a warm blanket, slippers, a silk eye mask over her closed lids. The soothing thrum of jet engines propelling her over the sea.

"Bye," repeated Flora, already looking back at her screen.

Lee wanted to sit beside Flora, to embrace her and help her stop trying to be perfect, stop making herself invisible. But was she seeing Flora's pain, or projecting her own? Was this even about Flora at all? Words burned inside Lee—not words of love, but words of instruction.

"Take care of each other," she said—something a caring aunt should say, not something she actually felt.

They nodded politely, distractedly, dismissively.

Bye.

Lee stood in the hallway. She missed the sound of Charlotte's Greek game shows that played too loudly every afternoon. When Lee had asked her mother if she should go back to California, Charlotte had said yes.

"I'm not needed here," Lee had said.

Charlotte had said, "Yes, that's right. I'm proud of you, Lee. Maybe you can bring me to the Academy Awards!"

Lee knocked on Regan's door, but there was no answer. She peered in and saw her sister fast asleep. Lee knew that Regan was strong, stronger than she. She was already pulling out of her complicated mess, and Lee's will would leave her family with plenty of money. Flora could buy a new computer; Regan could return to Savannah if she wanted, or not; Isabelle could move to Manhattan.

This was it—the last time she'd see this place and these people. The pills weren't about ending despair anymore. They were about finally being honest—she'd been going through the motions for so long, she'd forgotten what it actually felt like to love. Quietly, she pulled Regan's door shut.

The only thing left was Yassus. One last meal for her friend. And then she could board her plane and solve the problem of being Lee Perkins once and for all.

80 ISABELLE

AUNTIE LEE HAD DEPARTED AND ISABELLE'S MOTHER WAS GETTING ready for the ballet—she was going with some other moms to see *Giselle* performed in the Odeon of Herodes Atticus open-air theater at the Acropolis. Even nerdy Flora was out for the night, meeting with her computer friends at a nearby café. The timing was perfect for Isabelle to sneak away to her first real modeling job.

The photographer, Spyros Alexandros, had sent her a DM via Instagram:

I would like to offer an artistic photography opportunity. Portfolio development for international modeling. Compensation provided.

Isabelle messaged back, and they arranged to meet at his home studio. Isabelle didn't mention the appointment to anyone, not even Anastasia. She told her mom she was going to the movies.

Spyros's mansion was a 1930s modernist masterpiece, all clean lines and floor-to-ceiling windows. He was handsome in a European way, with the kind of confidence that came from always being the most important person in the room.

"Wine?" Spyros offered, already pouring. "This is from my family's vineyard on Naxos. We'll need you relaxed for the shoot."

Isabelle accepted a glass. Spyros led her through rooms filled with antiques and artwork, his hand occasionally touching her lower back. She pulled out her phone and snapped a selfie—her blood-red dress perfectly positioned to show her prominent collarbones. She looked mysterious, elegant, like someone with secrets worth knowing.

She posted to her story, already anticipating the likes, the comments, the attention.

"Beautiful," Spyros said, watching her pose. "But now it is time to put the phone away."

"What?"

"My shoots require absolute focus."

Isabelle hesitated for just a moment before giving him her phone, ignoring a small twisting feeling in her stomach.

"The other models are already here," Spyros said, leading Isabelle deeper into the house. "You'll work with them initially. Team shots—professional, artistic. OK?"

Isabelle nodded. Maybe it was OK. Yearning to be seen and a small bit of fear made her chest hot. Her breath was short. *Just nerves,* she told herself.

In the dining room, a long walnut table was set with crystal and silver. White roses and olive branches served as a centerpiece. About a dozen young women were already seated—all beautiful, all trying hard to look older than they were. Isabelle didn't recognize anyone.

The girls looked glassy-eyed. And the men around the table—older men with expensive clothes and predatory smiles—did not look like photographers or crew. They were holding wineglasses. They were watching. Something felt off. Isabelle could barely get a breath in. Her lungs were tight.

"Yet another model," said a brunette who looked about fifteen—but she couldn't be fifteen! There was no way. "Sit down, new girl."

Spyros stood behind a chair at the head of the table. Isabelle

sat, and he placed his large, cold hands on her shoulders as someone took a photo with a phone.

"You're gorgeous," he murmured near her ear, his breath
warm and smelling of cigarettes. "The camera loves you already."

Could Isabelle's wine be making her dizzy? Spyros offered her
a cigarette, and she accepted it and a light from his match.

"Tell me about your family," Spyros said, refilling her glass.
"Your mother, your father, they are Greek?"

"No," Isabelle paused, her mind feeling fuzzy. "My mom is
American. She's going through some things right now. Midlife
crisis stuff."

"Ah, yes. Women of a certain age." His smile was sympa-
thetic, understanding. "It must be difficult, being mature while
surrounded by . . . instability."

Isabelle smiled. "Yes," she murmured. "It *is* difficult." Spyros
didn't know the half of it, although Isabelle's mom really was trying to be normal. Isabelle forgave her mom—of course she did—
but a hot fury remained in Isabelle's body. There was nowhere for
the anger to go . . . Isabelle hoped it would somehow vanish.

Around the table, the other girls laughed nervously and fidg-
eted while the men—men in their thirties and forties and fifties—
watched them creepily.

"You should try this," the brunette said, sliding a small silver
tray toward Isabelle. White powder arranged in neat lines. "It
helps with nerves. For the shoot."

Isabelle hesitated for just a moment. She'd taken drugs with
Anastasia, but this was different. She was alone here, and she
didn't know what was in the powder.

"I don't want to pressure you," Spyros said smoothly. "Only if
you're comfortable. Though I think you'll find it enhances your
performance."

Isabelle leaned forward, following the brunette's example, feeling a burn, an immediate rush. The room became brighter, sharper. Her tongue felt loose, her body electric. She belonged in rooms like this.

Ah, thought Isabelle, tagging Atelier Nyx and its impressive address, *so this is what power feels like.*

"Much better," Spyros said, his hand finding her thigh under the table. "Now we can begin."

81 FLORA

FLORA STARED AT HER SISTER'S INSTAGRAM STORY: ISABELLE IN A red dress at some fancy house. Isabelle looked beautiful. Sophisticated. But something in her sister's eyes looked fake, as if Isabelle were an actress who was too scared to play her starring part.

Flora analyzed the outfit she had worn to meet her friends for an early coffee. Round glasses, hair in a boring ponytail, wearing a T-shirt and jeans that screamed *Loser!* No wonder no one noticed her other than the White Hat Hackers. There was nothing to see. Flora frowned. She went to change into her pajamas, then changed her mind.

Flora decided to track the address from where Isabelle had posted the photo of herself with her hand on her hip, like she belonged in a world of wealth and privilege. Well, if one Willingham sister belonged, the other could, too.

Flora threw open Isabelle's closet and found a tight black miniskirt and a sequined tube top. She yanked them on, took off her glasses, squinted at her reflection. Better.

She found Isabelle's makeup bag and started experimenting— foundation to even out her skin, mascara to make her eyes look bigger, lipstick in a shade called Midnight Rose that made her mouth look huge. Flora had watched Isabelle use her curling iron hundreds of times, but doing it herself was different. She burned her finger twice before getting the hang of it, but eventually her straight hair fell in soft waves around her shoulders.

The girl looking back at her was a stranger—someone who might actually belong at a party in Psychiko. She grabbed Isabelle's leather jacket and exited the apartment, feeling both terror and excitement.

Isabelle had posted from a mansion with iron gates and manicured gardens. This wasn't a bunch of kids—this was a serious adult gathering.

Flora almost turned around. Almost got back on the metro and went home to her homework and the empty apartment and her invisible, safe existence. But the thought of spending another night without anyone to talk to, the good girl who never got chosen—it made her walk all the way to the mansion's front door and ring the bell.

A man answered—older, with the kind of smile that made her skin crawl even as she tried to return it. "You are looking for Spyros?" he said in accented English.

Flora nodded.

"You are a bit late but it's OK. You are eighteen, my dear?" Flora nodded again, hoping he didn't ask for ID.

She was finally somewhere that mattered.

He led her through rooms that belonged in a museum, past other men who looked at her with expressions she couldn't quite read but that made her pull Isabelle's jacket around herself. The living room was full of girls who looked like models, beautiful and completely at ease, smoking.

Where was Isabelle?

"Wine?" A man appeared beside her with a glass already full. "Welcome dear. I'm Spyros. You look like you could use something to relax. This wine is from my family's vineyard on Naxos."

The first sip made her cough. It was strong, bitter and sharp and nothing like the wine coolers she'd tried once in Savannah.

"It's an acquired taste." Spyros's smile was understanding, paternal. "But you seem mature for your age—I think you'll appreciate it."

Mature. The word sent a thrill through Flora.

"You're very quiet," he said, settling into the chair beside her. "Thoughtful. I like that in a young woman. Still waters run deep, as they say."

His knee brushed against hers, and Flora moved away instinctively. But there was nowhere to go—she was trapped in the corner. "I should probably find my sister," Flora said.

"Sister?" Spyros's eyes sharpened. "What's her name?"

"Isabelle. Isabelle Willingham."

Something flickered across his face—surprise, then calculation. "Ah. Yes. She's . . . working right now. But what's the rush? You've only just arrived."

Working?

Over the man's shoulder, Flora scanned for Isabelle's familiar face among the strangers. The house was bigger than she'd realized, with hallways leading to rooms she couldn't see.

"Maybe you'd like to audition too?" he said.

"Audition?"

He touched her face and gazed at her. Flora had never wanted to be invisible more in her entire life. But it was too late.

82 LEE

LEE SETTLED INTO HER FIRST-CLASS SEAT. SHE TUCKED HER SHOES in the little pocket to the left of her feet. In the storage cabinet to her right, she put her pills. She took rosemary-scented hand lotion from the amenity kit and rubbed it into her fingers, then applied the tiny lip gloss and pulled an airplane-logo pen from its plastic bag. She considered writing something down, but in the end couldn't come up with anything to say.

Lee scrolled Instagram mindlessly, hunching low in her seat—she didn't want to be recognized. She spotted a story posted by Isabelle and touched her thumb to the screen to watch her niece's latest inappropriate, borderline-pornographic snapshots: a selfie of Isabelle in a low-cut dress, posing with a grown man at least Lee's age. Lee shook her head: She knew the look on Isabelle's face—the preening need to seem older than she was. And the guy looked like bad news for sure.

Lee stared at the photos—Isabelle posed and overeager, trying to seem sophisticated. It was like looking at her teenaged self, learning to weaponize beauty before understanding the cost. Had Lee taught Isabelle this? Had she shown her niece that being desired was the same as being loved?

Lee texted Regan: Isabelle just posted a worrisome Instagram. Do you know where she is?

The message showed "Delivered" but not "Read."

"Goddamn it," Lee muttered.

She called Regan.

Straight to voicemail. She remembered that Regan had been planning a ladies' night at the ballet, and must have turned off her notifications during the performance.

Lee tried Flora, then Isabelle.

Both phones were off. Now this was unnerving—the girls were never, *ever* offline.

Lee inhaled. She had done her part! She was ready to escape this family and this world. Still, Flora turning her phone off was especially strange. Lee opened her Find My app, as Flora had shown her how to do.

Flora had disabled her Find My app.

Lee stood and gathered her things.

"Do you understand that once you step off this plane, you cannot return?" asked the perky bitch guarding the jet-bridge.

"Yes," said Lee.

On the way to the address where Isabelle had tagged her photo, a place called Atelier Nyx, Lee tried calling Regan one more time.

No answer. Bitterly, Lee hoped she was enjoying the hell out of *Giselle.*

The taxi reached a modernist mansion set back from the street behind high walls draped with bougainvillea. "I'll be right back," said Lee.

"Oréa oréa," said the driver.

Lee stepped from the car onto the narrow street. A gate stood slightly ajar, and Lee walked through, crossing cement tiles to reach the entranceway. From inside came the distant sound of classical music and a man's voice giving directions: "Perfect. Now turn your head slightly. Beautiful. Show me more."

What the hell? Lee pressed the doorbell.

Shuffling footsteps approached, followed by the metallic slide of a lock being disengaged.

The heavy oak panel swung inward. There he stood—the older man from Isabelle's Instagram post. He wore an Egyptian cotton shirt tucked into tailored trousers and no shoes. A Patek Philippe watch. Professional camera equipment hung around his neck. "Hi," said Lee. "I'm here to pick up my niece? Isabelle Willingham?"

"Of course," said the man in an overly smooth baritone. "Parakaló, come in. I'm Spyros Alexandros. I'm a photographer. We're having a little . . . artistic session tonight."

He led the way through a hallway lined with framed photographs—all young women in various states of undress, all with the same pick-me-please expression. Lee's gut tightened, thinking of skeevy, predatory Mr. Ragdale.

They passed a dining room where several too-young girls sat around a table with wineglasses, looking bored and drunk.

"Isabelle is just finishing up," said Spyros. "Would you like to see some of my work? I'm documenting the transition from girl to woman. It's quite . . . profound."

"No. Take me to Isabelle now."

From down the hallway, Lee heard the sound of a camera shutter clicking rapidly, accompanied by a male voice: "Gorgeous. You're a natural. Now look at me like you want something. Like you're hungry for it."

Jesus Christ. Lee knew she should dial 911, or whatever the Greek 911 was called. She pivoted, turning from Spyros and moving toward the man's voice. Through a partially open door, she saw a room set up like a professional studio—lights, reflectors, a backdrop. An older man wielded a camera. Next to him, a videographer. "Perfect," said the man behind the camera. "Now slip the shirt off your shoulders. Show me you're ready for this."

"Close set!" yelled Spyros from behind Lee. The door was thumped shut before Lee could get inside. "Don't jump to conclusions," said Spyros, his wrist tight on Lee's upper arm. "Art is complicated."

Lee pulled free and threw her shoulder against the door, mercifully unlocked. She wedged her way inside.

In the center of the room, Flora stood in her underwear, eyes pressed closed, her face a mask of effort to stay still. Lee could see strain in every line of her body.

Lee froze, witnessing Flora—the smart one, the overlooked one—trying to transform herself, desperate to be seen at any cost.

This was the moment she'd been hurtling toward, the reason she'd never been able to rest, the danger Lee had always known was going to come.

Flora was performing for love, just like her Auntie Lee. Depression's voice roared in Lee's head: *You can't save her. You'll make it worse. You always make it worse. Just go.*

But something stopped her from leaving, something quiet and simple. She just . . . loved Flora. Flora—a young woman who mattered.

Lee walked toward her niece.

The photographer moved to block her path. "You're trespassing. Security!"

Lee heard footsteps approaching fast. "Flora, we're leaving."

Flora's eyes snapped open. She saw Lee and immediately tried to cover herself, humiliation flooding her face. "Auntie Lee! I— this isn't—"

"She signed a contract," the photographer said, clutching Flora's shoulder. "She can't just—"

"Let go of her." Lee's voice was deadly quiet. "Or every tabloid in the world will know exactly what Spyros Alexandros does with underage girls."

The photographer's grip loosened slightly, but he didn't release Flora. Spyros and another man entered the room. "Flora, you don't have to do this," Lee said simply. Not angry or dramatic. Just true.

"But I—he said I could be—"

"You're perfect." Lee's voice was steady. "And I love you."

Flora's façade dissolved completely, revealing the scared sixteen-year-old underneath. The photographer finally let go of Flora's arm, and she pulled on her tiny sequined top, stepped into her skirt and tugged it up to cover her thighs.

"She's here voluntarily. She wants this," said the photographer, stepping between Lee and her niece.

Lee looked at him with deadly calm. "She's sixteen. Get out of my way."

"The drama is unnecessary," said Spyros, approaching. "The girls are exploring their artistry—"

"I know exactly what this is." Lee's voice was quiet but powerful. She knew this script. She held up her phone, already recording. "And so will everyone else if you don't move. Now."

The men exchanged glances. Spyros muttered something in Greek to the photographer, who stepped aside. When Flora was dressed, Lee extended her hand.

Flora looked at it, then at Lee, but kept her arms wrapped around herself.

Lee nodded, accepting.

Flora nodded back, and together they moved toward the door.

Isabelle was smoking and sipping wine in the dining room. As they walked past, Lee paused, and Isabelle stood, spoiling for a fight. "We're going home," said Lee. "Are you coming?"

"No."

"Suit yourself," said Lee. "I love you."

Something changed in Isabelle's defiant expression—exhaustion making her shoulders fold inward. "Fine," said Isabelle. She set down her glass sharply. "Fine, I'll come."

They walked out together, Lee between the girls.

Spyros and two other men blocked their path. "This is a misunderstanding," he said. "The girls came here willingly. They wanted—"

Lee held up her phone, still recording. "Smile for my millions of Instagram followers."

The men exchanged glances. One muttered in Greek.

"You're making a mistake," Spyros said quietly. "I have lawyers. I have friends in—"

"As do I," Lee lied, her limbs trembling but her voice steady. "I'm expected on set tomorrow. If I don't show up, my director knows exactly where I was tonight."

A long moment passed. Finally, Spyros stepped aside.

In the taxi, Lee said, "Drive. Fast."

Through the rear window, she saw Spyros on the street, phone pressed to his ear, watching their car merge into traffic.

"Are they following us?" Flora whispered.

"No," said Lee. There were no headlights behind them. Not yet. "I won't leave tonight," said Lee. Neither Flora nor Isabelle responded. The driver headed toward Plaka, the streets of Athens blurring past: neon pharmacy crosses, Orthodox churches with golden domes, walls covered in ancient and modern graffiti. Flora's breathing slowed. The pills were still in Lee's purse, but when

Depression said, *They're better with you gone,* Lee knew that this was wrong.

You hurt everyone you touch, said Depression.

Yet there was Lee—Auntie Lee—safe, alight, moving within the luminous currents of a city she had come to love. Isabelle rested her head on Lee's shoulder, heavy and warm. Lee found Flora's hand in the dark. Flora opened her damp palm, and Lee held on.

EPILOGUE

ONE YEAR LATER
Ikaria Island, Greece

LEE STOOD ON THE STONE TERRACE OF PAROS'S HOME, WATCHING her family in the courtyard below. Charlotte was adjusting Paros's linen shirt, laughing at something he'd whispered as he tended the dying embers of the Easter fire. Flora sat on a woven mat with her laptop, but she kept looking up, checking that everyone was still there.

(They were all still there.)

Isabelle leaned against an ancient olive tree, no phone in sight. (Anastasia spent every Easter on the Boosalises' private island; she and Isabelle had flown to Greece from Brooklyn, where they shared an apartment in a doorman building in Bushwick.) Cord and Giovanni lounged on a wooden bench, both of them drowsy from the warmth of the Mediterranean sun. And Regan—Regan was sketching something in a small notebook, her movements assured, capturing the Byzantine church's bell tower in the distance.

It is, in a way, a miracle they are all here, Lee thought, and not just because uniting the Perkins family for Easter on Ikaria Island seemed insane, expensive, and possibly disastrous. Every one of them had almost vanished—Charlotte into her lonely Triscuit dinners, Cord into work and booze, Regan into a fantasy that almost swallowed her whole. Isabelle had been shrinking toward an image of starved perfection; Flora tried her best to disappear.

Lee had been the closest to gone. All those pills saved up, her plans to exit somewhere over the Atlantic. Now she slipped her feet from her sandals to feel warm stone underneath her. Her medication made her hands shake slightly. She felt duller, less sparkly, than when she was manic. But this was the price of being here, breathing in the scents of herbs and sea salt.

Lee's phone buzzed in her pocket—surely it was Francine, pestering her about the awards campaign for her star turn in *Mad, Bad, and Dangerous to Know*. Lee silenced it without looking. Whatever Lee decided about returning to Los Angeles, it could wait.

Lee had messaged Markos to let him know she was coming to Greece for Easter. They had stayed in touch after Lee couldn't stop worrying about Yassus—she'd asked Markos to check on him. Markos had not only found the big dog—he had brought Yassus home and adopted him. When Markos asked if Lee wanted to visit Yassus and have a home-cooked dinner before she caught her flight back to Los Angeles, Lee said yes.

Below her, Charlotte caught Lee's eye and raised her glass in a toast. Paros had his arm around her mother's shoulders, and Charlotte looked older and fragile but calmer somehow—maybe she was finally (at eighty-three years old) herself. Lee descended the stone steps. She pulled up a chair next to Flora, who leaned against her. "Did you take your—" said Lee.

"Yes," said Flora. "Did you take your . . ."

"Yes," said Lee. They took the same prescriptions in different doses.

"Γειά σου," Paros said, raising his glass.

"Yassou," they echoed. Lee had lost her drink, and when Regan held her glass out, smiling, Lee took a sip of her sister's wine. Growing quiet, they gazed at the darkening sky.

"I have an announcement," said Giovanni, breaking the silence. Cord stood up next to Gio.

"Mark your calendars, everyone," said Cord. Lee could barely recognize this gleeful, tanned version of her brother.

"Next summer . . ." said Giovanni.

"On the beautiful *Flying Star* sailing ship . . ." interjected Paros.

"They're getting married!" cried Charlotte, unable to cede the spotlight.

"Finally," said Cord. "And we hope you'll all join us, and Gio's family, too. It's going to be the wedding of the summer."

"Of the *century*, honey!" said Giovanni.

"Oh, Cord," said Lee, moving to embrace her brother, "you deserve this."

"I know," he answered, whispering, "So do you, Lee Lee."

"Hug me, too," said Giovanni. Lee's nieces and sister piled on. Charlotte stood aloof, but smiled. In the midst of her dysfunctional family, Lee closed her eyes, allowing happiness . . . and with it, the terror of having happiness taken away.

When Lee came back to herself, opening her eyes, Regan was standing before her. They'd barely spoken in the past year. Lee had told herself they were just busy. She mourned knowing her sister all the same. Regan was holding something—a small collage, maybe twelve inches square. "I made this for you," Regan said, not meeting Lee's eyes.

Lee took the artwork.

Against a background of four city maps—Savannah, Los Angeles, New York, and Athens—Regan had layered fragments of images: Isabelle fixing Flora's hair for her prom. Flora in her room, laughing during one of her evening video chats with Lee.

Charlotte holding a pistachio ice cream cone toward Regan. Cord taking a pause on a hike midway to the Acropolis for Giovanni to apply sunscreen to his nose. Paros in an apron, roasting lamb; Charlotte next to him, chopping vegetables. Lee herself, not cut from a magazine but a photo from someone's phone—hair messy, no makeup, feeding Yassus. And an old picture of Lee, Cord, and Regan at a long-ago Easter egg hunt, all of them dressed up for church. Charlotte didn't like frivolity on Easter, so Lee remembered the day vividly: the taste of jelly beans, the feel of cool grass on her bare legs. Lee touched the image of her younger siblings, cross-legged on a lawn, watching Lee intently as she evenly doled her own plastic, candy-filled eggs into their baskets.

"Do you get it?" asked Regan.

Lee nodded. She did get it.

"I'm trying to say . . . I'm sorry."

"I'm sorry, too."

"I wanted to be seen, I guess. But I forgot . . ." Regan gestured to her intricate collage, the photos arranged to tell a story. The most important story, thought Lee, and easy to lose sight of: It was small acts of love that kept you in the world.

The End

ACKNOWLEDGMENTS

The first glimmers of a novel are hopeful—characters come to me and I follow them and every time I tell you I think it will be easy. But then the stories go haywire, my obsessions are diverted by other obsessions, my fictional characters go on the lam, and life knocks me upside the head and I realize that what I think is the most important thing in the world to be writing about is a big illusion, even nuts—I must begin again, and better, because this novel will be the best novel ever—at last I will change the world with words. What keeps me from giving up is remembering the girl I used to be, at peace in the Rye Free Reading Room or in my grandparents' guest room on Belted Kingfisher in Hilton Head Island. All that girl wanted was an author with a story—Carolyn Keene, Judy Blume, Enid Blyton, and as I grew up: Paul Bowles, Raymond Carver, Denis Johnson, Tess Gallagher, and Gabrielle Zevin. I remember that girl with beaded barrettes and I write for her, to transport her, to get her out of herself.

All of this to say: I am grateful for the people who surround me and keep me sane, peaceful, inspired, and safe. Every minute I know I am lucky to have the love of Dr. Tip Meckel, my Numero Uno, my moonshot, the King of Rae Dell, El Capitan.

Thank you, T, for your tireless scientific work to save the planet and for the rosebush outside my writing cottage.

My beloved A, H, and N listen to all my crazy ideas, help me plan romance scams, heists, and adventures, and give me all the joy. Watching you three grow up is the best thing in the world.

Thank you to the fighters and artists of Austin, Texas: the LLL, the BHE crew, the Texas Book Festival team, the lifesaving T1D Mom Chat, the Small Carpool Superstars, my magazine editors, the fearless leaders and members of Girl Scout Troop 42908, my badass Hollywood mentors May Cobb and Chandler Baker; Erin and Tim Kinard; Mo and Stefan Pharis; Liz and Andy Gershoff; and Julio Rangel, who is serving the best pizza and Italian food in town at his Giovanni's Pizza Stand, located inside Chevron #382928.

Outside of the great state of Texas, thank you to Beth Howells (and our OG DBC), the fast girls of Kent '90, my travel writing editors and friends (especially Tykesha Burton, Joey Skladany, and Naomi Tomky), Jardine Libaire, Owen Egerton, Roslyn Gillespie, Dalia Azim, all the members of the magical Reese's Book Club chat—see you at ShineAway 2026!—the Hello Sunshine team, especially Jane Lee, Gretchen Schreiber, Olga Khaminwa, Ashley Rappoport, Kristin Perla, and the most luminous bookworm in the world, Reese Witherspoon. Shoutout to Laura Namey for reading this very novel and helping me fix it. Thank you to my shining new manager, Jordan Cerf; my whip smart film agent, Mary Pender; and the magnificent team at Ballantine Books: Kara Welsh, Jennifer Hershey, Kim Hovey, Taylor Noel, Emily Isayeff, Chelsea Woodward, Megan Whelan, Pamela Alders, Angela McNally, Andy Lefkowitz, Debbie Glasserman, Elena Giavaldi, Jeanne Reina, Jesse Shuman, and Michael Harney.

Thank you to my agent, Michelle Tessler, who encourages every strange idea I send her, and whom I love.

My editors Kara Cesare and Gabby Colangelo made a wild mess of pages into a novel. Thank you both for your insightfulness, brilliance, and creative inspiration, and for taking a chance on my next project. . . .

And, as always, sending all the love to my family—the Westleys, McKays, Bennigsons, Meckels, Toans, Wards, and Shabers.

AMANDA EYRE WARD is the *New York Times* bestselling author of ten novels, including *The Jetsetters,* a Reese's Book Club pick. She lives in Austin, Texas, with her family.

amandaward.com
X: @amandaeyreward
Instagram: @amandaeyreward